# RONDA

## 'Past and Present Colliding'

Teena Joyce

With lots of love

Teena Joyce x

Published by New Generation Publishing in 2021

Copyright © Teena Joyce 2021

First Edition

ISBN 978-1-80369-167-1

**www.newgeneration-publishing.com**

 New Generation Publishing

# 'RONDA'

## Back In the day

Ronda Simpson was born on July 13th, 1958 at Holbeach Maternity Hospital to a loving couple Ernest and Joyce Simpson who lived with their family in the small fenland, market town of Spalding in Lincolnshire.

Teena Joyce the author of 'Ronda - Back in the Day,' tells you how Ronda had a happy childhood as memories are shared with past and present colliding.

Over the decades, Ronda's fears of losing the most precious person in her life grew, until one day she tragically did. 'Read Back in the day,' as you are taken on a life time journey to the year 2000.

*Lesley*
Brilliant, brilliant, brilliant, what a truly wonderful read it was, I can't wait to read present day, you make Ronda's story full of interest, from page one I couldn't put it down - keep writing you truly have the gift.

*Valerie*
I love the way you managed to incorporate some humour through some of Ronda's saddest and most challenging times. It was a page turner; I didn't want the book to end. I am so happy that you are writing a second novel Ronda, 'Present day.'

*Alison*
Oh, what a good story teller you are, I have been hooked from page one, I have cried, I have laughed and

raised a few eyebrows. Loved the memoirs too, it was so nice to share those with your readers. Keep writing.

*Erica*
I cried at page three, laughed at page eighty-four. Fantastic read so far.

*Kev*
Sad to begin with, but further on she just has you rolling around in laughter.

Ronda remains living in her home town of Spalding in Lincolnshire with her family.

Read the most recent challenges Ronda has had to face over the past two decades in – 'Past and Present Colliding by Teena Joyce.

# 'RONDA'

## Past and Present Colliding.

### Acknowledgements and thanks

Special thanks to my husband Trevor for all the Love, Support and Care that he has given me for almost five decades. I could never have got here without you holding me up each time that I fell. You have been my rock, my angel and my forever best friend throughout the time since I met you.

And the never-ending support from the ladies from Ovarian Cancer UK, you are all so special and so, so brave. Love to all those who make it and the ones long gone – I think it would be fair to say the strong bond we have together has been simply awesome from the first day I joined the group. Stay safe and remember we can't be brave all the time, keep drying those tears, pulling up those big girl knickers and Fuck Cancer!

Thanks to Mary Mann for the long hours, she spent proof reading . . . and putting me on the straight and narrow, after her tips on writing my first story, made Ronda's follow up story from past and present colliding, possible, Thank you.

# The Chapters.

1) Past and Present Colliding
2) Dressed to Kill.
3) The Departure Lounge
4) The Syndrome - 2000
5) Fibro Fog
6) A Big Ask - 2000
7) You May Well Laugh - 2008
8) Ronda's Story
9) 3$^{rd}$ November - 2010
10) The Following Days - November
11) Recovery
12) Chemotherapy
13) The WIG
14) BRCA
15) GERD
16) The Highway Code.
17) Here Again 2019
18) 1$^{st}$ February - 2021
19) The Grim . . .
20) Intimacy.
21) Results
22) Wednesday 11$^{th}$ August - 2021
23) Chocolate Cheesecake
24) One day at a time.
25) Thursday 2$^{nd}$ September 2021
26) Thursday 16$^{th}$ September 2021
27) A Surprised phone call 2021

# Chapter 1

## 'Past and Present Colliding'

In the early seventies, Ronda's best friends were the two Susans and Diana.

The first Susan moved schools when Ronda did, but they were separated into different classes. Susan always had her wits about her, she was put in the 'A' stream, Ronda was put in the 'C.' She couldn`t understand why, she had worked really hard during the last year but I guess the previous years also counted for a lot. The then eleven-year-old Ronda was gutted, Susan and herself had made a pact that best friends should stay together forever and ever.

During the 1969 summer holidays they played together every single day that they could: inseparable they were. They spent their Saturday afternoons in Ayscoughfee gardens along with a lot of kids of the day. At two thirty in the afternoon they would meet up with a couple of lads at the band stand. Richard and William used to come all the way from Holbeach on the bus to meet them.

Towards the end of the summer, they failed to turn up and they were never to be seen or heard from again. I guess that was their first romance over and done with. It would have been nice if they could have met them in Holbeach`s Carters Park and walk the short distance to buy a Laddies Ice cream, but their parents wouldn't hear of it and they knew there would be no point to mither about it, because once they had said NO, they knew they wouldn`t waver.

The two girls never even considered what would happen if they were separated into different classes, but at least they still had their Wednesday night dancing classes to look forward to, they always spent their Saturday afternoons together. But at school, Susan had made lots of new friends and Ronda felt lonely, there wasn`t one other single person from the Parish Church Day school in her class.

Ronda had started ballet class at the age of four, the lessons were held at Ayscoughfee hall. It is now a museum of the Fens, including a dead mummified cat that must be hundreds of years old. The dark parquet floor remains just the same, and the original floor to ceiling dance mirrors are still mounted on the wall, the only difference in present day, is Ronda's reflection looks very different now, as some of the years have not been kind.

By 1969 Ronda, Susan and Diane went to the same dance class, they were part of the amateur dramatic society, taking part in Bless the Bride, Student Prince, Oklahoma and the final year the pantomime, Aladdin, for which they were under contract - they actually got paid for that one.

Ronda`s mother, Joyce made the costumes for the three girls, on the original singer sewing machine, which was the most sophisticated machine back in the day - other dancers would have had them made. I think Joyce would have been happy enough to make them all had they given her more time.

Ronda hung out with the other Susan too sometimes, but because her mother worked, that Susan spent a great deal of time at her Nan's who lived in Moulton Chapel, hardly walking distance from Spalding. The second Susan and Diana were a little younger than Ronda and the big Susan, so they had another year at the Parish Church Day school before they started the Gleed Girls' school.

Five decades on and Ronda can still remember her friends' telephone numbers, the first Susan's number was 3476 and the second Susan's was 4110. She didn't call Diana very often because invitations to play were usually made by their mothers, so she doesn't remember her number.

In the here and now of 2021 Ronda and the first Susan are back in touch after their own daughters became adult friends, through Ronda and Susan's grandchildren. It's a small world but so many years lost. It's life though isn't it? We grow up, get married, have children, return back to work and our paths had never crossed for many a good year. It's really special that children become friends from one generation to the next.

And yes, they will be reading this book . . .

One of Ronda's many new class friends, Beverley Smith, emigrated to South Africa around 1972. They had also previously met at the Fenland Tappers a different dance class to Mary Alan's school of dance which was where the other girls went. Fenland Tappers was run by Greta, the very Greta who became Ronda's mother's best friend.

In the holidays the girls spent many a happy day apple scrumping over Two-Plank Lane that led into Gowt Lane. When Beverley left the UK with her parents the two friends stayed in touch through pen and paper, they had no internet or face book to keep in touch, no mobile phones and such like. Letters took weeks to arrive, and back in the day they wrote on special air mail paper that was like writing on Izal toilet paper. Then it folded and sealed into the shape of an envelope, there was always very little space to write so the letters could only be short. But the girls were good at keeping in touch, and each time Beverley came back to Spalding to see her Nan and Granddad, she always made an effort to surprise Ronda with a visit round Cardigan House.

By 1981 Ronda and Billy had been married four years and their first daughter had been born. Beverley didn't marry until a few years later, in the meantime she kept writing and continued to visit Ronda at Matmore Close, which was her marital home for twelve years.

Then Beverley met and married a handsome helicopter pilot within six weeks of meeting him, he whisked her off to Austria to live with his parents while he continued to fly to faraway places. She could not speak a single word of German and his family were not bilingual. Times were tough for her and she wrote to Ronda every single week claiming how miserable she was. But she was made of tough skin and knuckled down until she was fluent in speaking German, even with the Vorarlberg accent.

The two friends were delighted to announce they were pregnant and due around the same time, Ronda with her second daughter and Beverley with her first.

Beverley and her baby came to visit the Grandparents who still lived in Weston, but Ronda and her children saw them every single day without fail. It was dreadful having to part when it was time for Beverley to return to her husband.

The following year in 1986 Ronda and Billy flew to stay with Beverley and Erich in their ultra-modern and spacious flat in Austria. This opened up a whole new chapter of events that left some laughable moments.

Ronda and her family boarded the train at Peterborough railway station to set off for their three-week adventure. At first it opened up Ronda's memory box, as her thoughts drifted off to a far-off place within her own childhood, the compartments that seated six passengers remained exactly how Ronda had remembered them, with walnut trims to the upholstery of dark red fabric, that had by then seen better days, with the same overhead luggage racks. The diesel train didn't quite smell the same as the older steam train had, and they didn't have the silver served breakfast like she remembered as a child - the first time she had ever tried toast and real butter and orange marmalade with the sticky orange peel slices. It was served in a polished silver jam jar with a dolly sized matching silver spoon. She remembered how large the knife and forks were, and the sugar lumps like the ones the doctor put the nasty tasting medicine in; The matching silver milk jug and teapot, a second pot of boiling water to top up the teapot; the silver tea strainer like Mummy`s although without the tea stains; the crisp white table cloth and matching napkins that were as large as a hand towel. She recalled the red leather that stuck to the backs of her legs when she wore her ankle socks in the summer.

They shopped in Harrods, Selfridges, Hamley`s and Fortnum and Mason's. They watched the change of the Queens Guards outside Buckingham Palace.

They went to Madam Tussauds, the art galleries, enjoyed a tour of the sites of London on the red open top double-decker bus. They went over Tower Bridge; they saw Big Ben. They took a boat trip along the Thames. They fed the pigeons in Trafalgar Square. They went up the Post Office Tower. Each visit they saw something new for the first time until they had exhausted the whole city.

They went to the London Palladium to see a show, they went to the Royal Albert Hall, after Ronda's first holiday to Austria. Ronda and her mother wore traditional Austrian costumes to watch traditional Austrian dance and folk music. They looked divine in the fabrics Ronda's mother had transformed into homemade costumes from traditional Austrian fabrics bought the previous summer in Kitzbhel on the Austrian Tyrol.

Ronda`s thoughts were jolted back to 1986 as they came into Kings Cross station.

Lugging a five-year-old, baby, pushchair and two very heavy suitcases on and off the train was no joke, getting down the steps from Kings Cross station to the underground to catch another train to the airport was even more stressful. Ronda felt the same terror as she had experienced when she was a child herself: the hum of the train, the way it wafted cold air as it came to a stop. How quickly everyone panicked to board once others had got off. The doors seemed to close far too quickly. It made Ronda just as anxious now as it had done over a decade ago. What if Billy and her got separated? Or even worse, what if they left one of the children behind? Or what if their cases went before they had time to board the train themselves, they'd have no clothes for their holiday? Ronda's mind was running out of control.

'Focus, focus,' she kept telling herself!

Ronda was rather surprised as well as relieved when the train came out of the darkness of the tunnel and back into the sunshine. The tension seemed to relax a little until the train came to a stop at the airport, then they had the same kerfuffle getting off the train, as they did getting on it. All Ronda kept thinking was, never again! Little did she know the nightmare of a journey had only just begun.

There must have been a lift but they never found one. No one got off the train and the whole platform was eerily empty, the train hummed and sped into the distance while the draught settled.

'You must be joking,' Ronda told her husband as she stood at the bottom of the moving escalator.

'Is that the only way up?' she asked.

'It'll be fine,' Billy told his wife with more confidence than she had.

While Ronda stood at the bottom with the children, she

watched her husband put one suitcase on the moving stairs, he took it off and left it unattended at the top of the stairs while he came back down on another escalator. He repeated this performance until all the luggage sat at the top waiting for them. It really was a blessing there wasn't a soul about. That said, had there been maybe they would have had help.

Ronda should have listened and waited for Billy to take the pushchair and one of the children. Instead, she attempted to do it all on her own, as if it wasn't a skill in itself to get on and off one of those things in high heels, let alone with a pushchair, a toddler and a five-year-old. Everything would have been okay if Lizzie hadn't panicked and refused to get on. As Ronda leant backwards to grab her, the heel in her shoes got caught in one of the grids, she lost her balance and fell on top of little Lizzie, with pushchair and eighteen-month-old Bella sandwiched on top. Lizzie was screaming blue murder, insisting her mother had killed her and accused her accordingly.

Everything after that, seemed to happen so fast - it was surreal how quickly the escalator stopped moving and the paramedics were helping them up. Lizzie was being hysterical and her mother shaken, Ronda had lost the heel of her shoe. They all had a medical health check to make sure they were fit to travel. Apart from a few scratches and bruises, they were fine, and they were safely escorted to the check in desk. The family felt much better for getting rid of their luggage, and now their holiday could begin.

Ronda left Billy with the children while she took

herself off to the duty free to buy the perfume, she had been saving for. There was a long queue to pay and then the till broke down and they didn't have any change. By the time the girl had come back with some change the family's flight was being announced ready to board. Everything would have been fine if Billy had stayed in the same place, but he decided to take the girls for a walk to look for their mother, and somehow they kept missing one another. It didn't seem long before the loud speaker announced their flight was waiting for a Mr. and Mrs. Stone and family to board the aircraft. Shortly followed by a second announcement to say the gates were now closing and the flight was getting ready for take-off. By this time Ronda had found her husband and they and the children were running as fast as they could towards the boarding gates, but their flight had already closed. They stood in shock, they had missed their flight by the skin of their teeth and there was nothing they could do about it. Then suddenly a gentle voice spoke from behind, 'It's ok, the plane won't fly itself.'

They turned, and met the actual pilot strolling along as though he had all the time in the world.

He took the pushchair from Billy and reassured him it could go in the front of the plane. 'But don't make a habit of it,' he joked.

As they were led to their seats by the pilot himself, he announced to the rest of the passengers 'I found them, so let's get this plane in the air,' and the other passengers, clapped and cheered.

Beverley and baby Rebecca was waiting to collect them as soon as they had landed in Zurich. They had a trouble-free journey in Bev's car to the other side of the border into Austria.

Beverley lived in the beautiful village of Nuziders in the Vorarlberg.

It was Billy`s first time in Austria, but it was just as pretty as Ronda`s memory when she was a twelve year old girl, the summer of 1970, with its quirky chalet type houses with balconies filled with an amazing display of red, pink and white geraniums and petunias. The scent was so refreshing, they were picture perfect and well maintained and cared for by their owners.

The small church rendered in white was ringing its bell on their arrival, a funeral may be! The grave yard was as polished and well cared for as the villagers' gardens. Each headstone was immaculately white and the flowers were as fresh as the day they were picked. Beverly said that each generation take care of the graves belonging to their ancestors, and at twilight candles would be lit. Ronda wanted to take a picture but Beverley said it was not permitted because it would be disrespectful. It was so peaceful and tranquil a tear rolled down Ronda's cheek as she thought of her mum. 'Tomorrow,' Bev promised, 'we can go into the church and light a candle for your mum,' That was typical Beverley, always thoughtful and kind.

. . . .

It was a hot day and although Beverley had a wonderful balcony that ran the full width of the apartment, it didn't have enough space for the three little ones to splash about in the paddle pool. There was a communal garden that the tenants could use. Rebecca had her own swing in it but it wasn't really suitable to kick a ball about.

However, right high up on the roof top was a flat concrete terrace where Bev had a washing line, a few deckchairs and sun loungers. Plus, Rebecca's paddle pool.

The building was owned by three middle aged sisters, Inga, Olga and Gertrude and their brother Rupert. On the ground floor was where they ran their family business making the most wonderful materials one could ever imagine. They used to give Beverley the off cuts so she could make Rebecca dresses, she also made traditional Austrian costumes for the three little girls. They looked so sweet all dressed the same when they went out to the beer festival in the village.

The sisters had also installed a sauna which was quite popular for the Austrians of that era. The sisters lived together in a four-bedroom apartment on the second floor. Their brother Walter, lived alone in one of the smaller apartments. A retired South African couple lived on the next floor, and then there was Beverly's family. So it was quiet and respectful and everyone shared and no one took advantage.

Beverley had become really good friends with the three older women and they all adored Rebecca because they had never married, so had no children of their own.

After dinner that evening and once the children were in bed, Inga knocked on the door to invite Ronda and Beverley to join them in the sauna. Beverley did warn that they always went into the Sauna naked. After several glasses of wine, followed by several shots of schnapps, the five women were rather giggly. Beverley was trying to translate every word the sisters said but was having difficulty keeping up, and the four of them were in hysterics. Ronda laughed as much as they did because although she couldn`t understand the half of it, they were just so funny. When they had sweated enough, they all screamed in an ice-cold shower, and ran out into the darkness of the night. 'Come on,' Bev beckoned, 'we have to keep up.'

'Where are we going?' Ronda asked still laughing.

'For a jog to dry off, I think,' Beverley chuckled.

'What naked?' Ronda questioned in surprise.

With that Beverley had gone and Ronda followed!

Bev and Ronda had left their husbands playing chess and drinking schnapps on the balcony above. The five giggling women ran round and round the garden in the altogether, shouting and waving to Billy and Erich above. But the two men were so engrossed with competing at chess they hadn`t got a clue about the goings on in the garden below. What a sight for sore eyes and they missed it all . . .

The siblings were having a huge modern home built on part of the garden but there was minimal noise from the workers.

On that first day Beverley and Ronda decided to stay close to home to give the girls a chance to recover after their journey, while Billy went with Erich for a helicopter tour of the alps. In the afternoon the two friends spent a couple of hours on the sun terrace while the three children enjoyed a splash about in the paddle pool.

'What on earth are you wearing?' Beverley asked her friend.

'Why?' Ronda demanded as she looked down at her lime green bikini.

'It looks like it belongs in another life,' Bev chided.

'Good job no bugger can see me up `ere then `init,' Ronda chuckled.

'I hope you have another one. We can't have you wearing THAT when we go to the big outdoor pool tomorrow.'

'I don't know what's wrong with it,' Ronda scoffed, because she really, really didn't.

'Well, for a start the bottoms are far too big for you and the top doesn`t show off enough cleavage.'

'It`s alright, no one is going to be looking at what I`m wearing.'

'Don`t you believe it mrs, with a figure like that, you need to flaunt it a bit. Have you only bought the one then?'

'Yup, it's the only one I have.'

`Well, you can borrow one of mine until we can get to the shops on Monday, keep your eye on Becs,' and with that she had gone.

On her return she dropped a bright cerise pink wincey-weeny-polka-dot-bikini in her lap.

'Go on then, try it on.'

'It doesn`t look as though it`ll leave a great deal to the imagination,' Ronda huffed.

Ronda dropped the shoulder straps and eased each arm out slowly, she reached her arms behind her to disconnect the hook and eye fastener and it dropped to the floor.

'Christ almighty, you breast fed two babies and have tits like that. Girlfriend, have you had a boob job?' Bev laughed out loud.

She proceeded to drop her panties to her ankles and stepped out of them, she stood completely naked and lathered herself in sun cream, which was something else she hadn`t thought to take with her – it was a good job her friend was organized.

Then they heard it, their men flying from a distance, thud, thud, thud from the helicopter as it flew over. Beverley, squealed in excitement, 'Look kids it's your daddies,' and they all started to wave furiously.

Ronda totally forgot about her nudity and joined in shouting and waving. Erich flew right over into the distance, then back, flying much lower the second time, for a better look. So much noise and commotion brought attention to themselves and once the thudding from the helicopter had faded into the distance it was taken over by wolf whistles, laughter and loud voices. Beverley, realized what was happening before Ronda, and she was laughing so hard she cried. Then Lizzie said, 'Mummy why have you taken your clothes off?' she started pointing and reciting 'Mummy is in the nudie; Mummy is in the nudie.' And the little ones started to chant with her.

As the penny dropped, Ronda was mortified. She had been totally oblivious about the fact the builders were roofing the sister's house and enjoying a bull's eye view of Ronda prancing about in her altogether.

It was a while before Ronda responded, she was far too

shocked to move or cover herself. Beverley was still laughing so hard she stopped breathing and the children joined in, pointing and giggling while the builders continued to whistle and shout!

They couldn`t say, 'get them off,' because she had already done that, what exactly they did shout was anyone`s guess, unless you spoke German. Beverley understood of course but she couldn`t possibly repeat it, there were little ones present. That said, it didn't stop them joining in the fun!

'Aunty Ronda has taken her clothes off, ha! ha! ha! Mummy has a bare bum; Mummy has a bare bum!'

Oh, my goodness, it was only their first day and already she had taken her clothes off - TWICE!

The weather was so hot the following day, the two friends took the girls to the open-air swimming baths, while Billy explored the Alps from the air with Erich.

The outdoor sports complex was like nothing in the UK because it was all outside. There was a variety of swimming pools: a baby/toddler pool, where most of the yummy mummies gathered; a sports pool, where a variety of water games took place such as water polo, and the pretty young ladies practised their synchronized swimming techniques; aqua aerobics and such like. Then there was the fun pool, with a wave machine and water slides. There was an adult pool for serious swimming or learners at different times of the day. And there was the very deep diving pool for the purpose of diving only.

Besides all of this there were changing rooms to get showered and dressed; hot food, cold food, snacks to eat in or take away, a coffee shop, tea rooms, ice cream stands, everything and anything you could think of. You could spend every day there for a week before getting round it all. They even had a beach wear shop, where Ronda could buy some new swimwear.

Mostly they just stayed close to the baby and toddler area. This was also where some of the fittest guys sunbathed as they goggled over the women. The area around the facilities had well kept lawns and gardens. There were deckchairs or sun loungers to hire for the day or you could just lay on your own towels or picnic blankets. You could also take in your own picnic which is what they did, because it was almighty expensive to eat there.

Ronda hadn`t noticed the group of fit blokes who sunbathed close by, but Beverley had because she overheard what they were saying, they were pretty loud and obviously German spoken, they continued to glance over laughing and larking about. Then Beverley hushed Ronda so she could catch what they were saying because they had by now become quite aware they were being talked about.

Of course, Beverley had lived in Austria long enough to speak fluent German she even used the local accent, not that Ronda would know the difference but other people did. She was so fluent most people assumed she had been born and bred there, although her dark brown hair and olive skin gave it away that she wasn`t pure blood.

The guys couldn't have heard her speak German, only English to Ronda and the children. For some reason these guys seemed to find that a bit of a challenge.

Anyway, Beverley had a plan.

'Come on,' she said, 'let's get the kids an ice cream, it's fun time.'

As they walked ever so slowly past these young men, one of them spoke loudly enough to be heard, Beverley turned her head to stare at him before talking loudly to the kids in English. Their typical male banter continued with more laughter as their testosterone took over their sensibility.

On the way back Beverley said, 'Now, I want you to do exactly what I tell you.'

'Listen,' she said, 'when we walk back past these guys, I am going to talk to you really loud in German so they can hear, then I want you to say 'Yah, Yah,' like this, 'Yah, Yah' that means you are agreeing to what I say.

'Okay,' Ronda agreed, 'but what are you going to say?'

'Never mind that, I will tell you later, because you must sound convincing and sound very stern and serious. Can you pull it off?'

'Yah, Yah,' she repeated while the two friends giggled like silly teenagers. The only problem was Ronda felt terribly stupid and couldn't help but laugh her head off.

As they passed the guys, they stopped chatting and fixed their stare on Beverley and Ronda, then they looked from one to the other and back again. Eyes looking each one of them up and down in unison. Beverley, spoke a loud gobble-dee-gee to her friend and Ronda quickly responded with a 'Yah, Yah.'

The look on these guys faces was a jaw dropping picture, as the girls both cracked up laughing to themselves.

Bev made Ronda wait until the children were in bed sleeping before she would tell her what the guys had been saying. That explained why Bev had asked Ronda if she would like to take their bags off in German!

# Chapter 2

## 'Dressed to Kill!'

Although Billy had never met Erich before their visit to Austria, the two chaps got along incredibly well. Erich delighted in introducing Billy to all his friends. By the end of the first week of their holiday they had been invited to various house parties, swimming pool parties, Braai's (what Beverley called a barbeque,) beer festivals with live music or local traditional dancing. This was when the children wore their traditional costumes that Beverley had made for them.

As you are probably aware by now Ronda did not drink - not after she had been on the receiving end of her father's drinking related abuse. However, it didn't take a lot to get high on sugar. Drinking on the night of the sauna was an exception and the following day Ronda suffered for it miserably. But there was this one time when they went for a English Braai with friends who insisted on taking the car keys off her because they thought she had one too many, 'as pissed as a fart,' was how they described her that evening. Truth be told all she had drunk was too much lemonade and a massive portion of Pavlova. Believe it or not, it was the truth.

Each table consisted of around twenty people, who sat on wooden benches either side of a very long table. Ladies clothed in traditional dress, filled their glass with beer from a jug, there was juice for the children. Ronda had the juice. Glasses were never empty for long and if they were still half full their maid, Marion, filled their glass to the top. As each table made merry, they swayed from side to side, swinging and sloshing their beer glasses one way, then the other, in unison.

A wonderful couple called Margo and Vernon had two young boys who were part of the dance group. It was interesting and fun. The boys wore traditional costume of lederhosen and white shirts with embroidered edelweiss on each corner of the collar. As long as the music played the dance troupe continued to dance, there was a lot of leg slapping and feet stomping as they spun one another round and they jingled their tambourines. They formed arches with their hands together, while other couples bent to skip under them. Then the dancing stopped while the music continued to play, the female dancers walked around the tables to choose a dance partner from the audience, while the male dancers each asked a lady to dance.

Ronda prayed and prayed when she noticed this young guy heading towards their table, 'Please don`t pick me, please don`t pick me,' she recited to herself in thought. She dared not look up, she looked the other way and kept her drink in her hand, taking little sips, to indicate she wasn't game for dancing. A hand appeared from behind her, he took her glass and placed it on the table in front of where she sat, then he took hold of her hand to lead her onto the dance floor.

'Oh no, sorry, I can't dance,' she told him, he didn't understand and he just kept grinning at her, like some sort of Cheshire cat. 'No, no,' she repeated, 'I don't want to dance,' Beverley was beside herself with laughing.

'Tell him Bev,'

'Tell him what?' she chuckled.

'Tell him bloody ANYTHING, tell him I can't dance because I have a back injury.'

Beverley laughed even more.

'Please, Bev, tell him, tell him, I have broken my toe, if you are my best friend, you will tell him.'

'In those high heels, he ain`t going to believe that honey!' she chided.

'Then tell him something else, I am grieving over my dead dog, any bloody thing.'

The more Ronda made a public display of herself the more everyone laughed.

The table of friends were all cheering and egging her on. What choice had she got? She felt another embarrassing situation about to engulf her.

Ronda was so nervous and when she is nervous, she talks too much.

'Do you speak English?' she asked.

'Yah, Yah,' he answered with a frown on his face as if she was plain stupid.

'Thank goodness for that,' she told him. 'At least you can tell me what to do.'

He grinned and nodded. 'Yah, Yah,' he said.

'Are my shoes too high?' looking down at her feet, he looked down too.

'I think maybe I should take them off, do you?'

'Yah, Yah,' he nodded.

So she kicked them off, and slid them to one side and the dancing began.

The man bowed to the lady, the lady curtsied back,

three steps to the left, three steps to the right. A hop and a skip forward, two steps back, they skipped in a circle, with two claps of the hand. Each couple joined hands and skipped forward while the man held her arm in the air and twirled her around.

The first couple joined hands to form an arch, while the second couple in line skipped under and joined hands to make a second arch. The third couple skipped under the two arches and formed a third arch on the end and so on, until there were six arches in total. Then the last couple went under the other five arches and skipped off. The next couple skipped under the four arches and skipped off, the next skipped under three arches and so on. Once the sequence had been completed all six couples finished with a very fast Polka.

Ronda did well, in fact she quite enjoyed herself UNTIL the music stopped and she was seeing double as every person spun around and around, laughing and clapping, voices were distorted to an echoed mumble. Ronda thought she was going to throw up. The second her dance partner let go of her hand to take his bow, she was supposed to curtsy but all she could do was wobble on her legs. Luckily, he caught her, he smiled and nodded but the instant he let her go she stumbled and fell in a heap on the floor. He kindly helped her up said something in German, let go and tried to walk away. She grabbed him, begged him to help her back to her seat. She could not stand let alone walk in a straight line. Everyone was laughing. Ronda thought she was going to die. She wasn't drunk, she was just dizzy, so bloody dizzy. But all she was, was everyone's joke, and Ronda wasn't laughing.

She stayed on the floor, and sat with her head between her knees until the dizzy spell and motion sickness passed and it did eventually. She crawled on her hands and knees to find her shoes, but she didn`t put them on. She staggered back to the table with smudged lipstick, hair looking like a mop, she was sweating all over and she wanted to go home.

'Oh my God,' Beverley said, 'you weren't wrong when you said you get pissed easily. How much of that fruit punch did you drink?'

'It`s not the drink, I had the same as the kids.'

'Not pissed,' Erich chided, 'you can`t even walk straight, and that's without the heels.'

'That's because I`m bloody dizzy, you numpty.'

'I`ll be ok, it's passing, I am just so hot and thirsty.'

Erich clicked his fingers at their maid Marian, and said something to her in German.

Minutes later she returned with a large jug of refreshing iced spring water.

Once Ronda had guzzled down her first glassful, she started to feel much better.

'Anyway,' Bev said, 'you seemed to be having a very amusing conversation with your dancing partner, didn`t you?'

'I may as well have not bothered, all he flipping did was laugh at every single bloody word I said, and I wasn`t saying anything particularly funny,' she scoffed.

'Ronda, you are always funny,' Billy told her.

'Well, maybe he didn`t understand English,'

27

Beverley told her.

'Oh, he could,' Ronda insisted, 'I asked him.'

'You asked him?' Bev queried.

'Yes, I asked him if he could speak English and he said, 'Yah, Yah,' Ronda explained.

'Well maybe he didn`t understand the question, if you asked him in English.'

'I didn`t ask him in English, I asked him in German,' Ronda told her friend.

'You asked him in German,' Beverly queried.

'I did,' she said proudly.

'So, what did you say exactly?' Bev wanted to know.

'I said, 'Do you speak English?' in German.'

'Tell us what you said in German?' Billy chuckled.

'Do I have to?' she asked like a scolded child.

'Yes, I am intrigued,' Bev laughed.

Ronda cleared her throat and said, 'Sprichst du Deutsch?'

AND EVERYONE LAUGHED OUT LOUD!

# Chapter 3

## 'The Departure Lounge.'

The three weeks went so fast - the two families had so much fun it was certainly an incredible holiday.

The evening before their departure, gathering things of importance together, Billy asked, 'Ronda, can I have the passports and return flight tickets?'

'The passports?' she questioned.

'Yes, the passports and the flight tickets.'

'What makes you so sure I have them?'

'Because I haven't, so you must have them.'

'Well, I dun know where they are, I haven't got them.'

'You have, I gave them to you on the flight out to put in your bag.'

'Did you,' she double stammered, 'I don't remember.'

'Well can you check please, instead of arguing the toss.'

Ronda remembered they flew out with Swiss-air because the plane lay out was different and the flight attendants wore a beautiful posh red uniform rather than the dull navy blue British Airways girls wore. She remembered the free colouring book and crayons the children got to amuse them on the flight, she remembered the small bottles of wine Billy and Ronda received free too. You never received free gifts from British Airways. She remembered the girls asking for their free gifts to show Rebecca when they arrived, she remembered snapping at the children in all the kerfuffle unpacking. She couldn't find her perfume that she had bought from the duty free either. After all that, she had lost it - HOW?

Well, the suitcase trolley they used to transport the luggage to the car park was unpacked into the boot of Beverley's car for the homeward journey to Austria. They could only assume the carrier bag with the free gifts and Ronda's fifty-pound bottle of perfume had been left on the trolley.

Oh-my-God, Ronda thought anxiously. When Billy handed her the passports and flight tickets before take-off, had she put them in the carrier bag with the perfume?

Time to confess . . .

Three weeks was a long time to remember and when Ronda had noticed the bag was missing, she was upset enough over the perfume, totally switched off about the importance of such documents to get back to the UK. To think they had almost missed their flight over that bottle of perfume, let alone lost the bloody documents to get home.

Ronda checked her bag, she also checked the hand luggage bag and the zipped compartments in both suitcases. She checked the bedside drawers her side to the bed. She double checked the chest of drawers where their clothes had been stored.
NOTHING!

'You don't seem to be in the least bit perturbed 'how'

the hell are we are going to get home tomorrow?' Billy scoffed.

'What are we going to do?' she cried.

'There is only one thing we can do and that's pray someone found them and handed them in.'

So he phoned the air-port in Zurich, 'No, I am sorry sir, there doesn't appear to be anything handed in I'm afraid, can you try again in the morning.'

'What were they going to do?'

They decided as their flight wasn't until late afternoon, they should get to the airport as early as possible the following morning and hope the documents had been found.

They all had a lousy night's sleep, tossing and turning with an over active mind was torturous. Ronda got up to make a hot drink, Beverley had been awake too and heard Ronda walking about in the living room. She joined her friend to offer a re-assuring hug. Always the optimistic one, Bev said, 'Listen dolly, it's not the end of the world, I mean if you miss the flight, we can book another and get the UK to send new passports to get you home if needs be.'

'Will they do that?' Ronda asked wiping her tears on the sleeve of her pyjamas.

'Of course,' Bev said with certainty 'People lose their tickets and passports all of the time, and at least you can stay here for as long as it takes, which has to be a good thing, doesn't it?'

'I suppose,' she said, with a faint chuckle.

'That's better,' her friend told her 'Less than twenty-four hours ago you were sad about leaving, and none of you wanted to go and now you are flipping balling because you can't get home, you are a one,' and Bev hugged her again.

Ronda felt much better, the two friends sipped their mugs of hot chocolate and slept much better until the early hours.

Erich had left for work before Billy had finished his shower, Beverley dropped Rebecca off at nursery at eight thirty that morning and then she drove Ronda and her family to Zurich, it was a couple of hours' drive. But they were there by ten thirty and their flight wasn't until four thirty in the afternoon.

They sat in the booking-in desk area close to Swiss-air, Billy checked every hour to see if the tickets had turned up. But another worry that concerned them was they hadn't even got their names on that flight back to London.

They anxiously sat for six long hours, it was costing a fortune on food, drinks and things to keep their little girls occupied.

By four o'clock the departure gates for their flight had long been open, but they stood no chance boarding, even if they did have their passports and flight tickets, they had no reserved seats according to the Swiss-air booking system. Just as they were going to give up and drive back to Austria, one of the attendants came over and asked if they had checked at the British Airways desk? They hadn't, it hadn't even crossed their mind, so Billy didn`t hesitate he ran like Billy- hell on four legs to the British Airways desk which was right the other end to where they had been waiting in the hope for some positive news.

Puffing and panting Billy started to urgently push past

passengers in the queue with apologies.

'Excuse me, may I squeeze past' it`s urgent,'

'Thank you, thank you,'

'Sorry may I push in,' It's a matter of great urgency.'

He asked so nicely, no one objected, apart from one big guy with a long beard and lots of tattoos that covered his arms and legs. He didn`t object but he offered a rather threatening look that made Billy apologise again and he couldn't thank him enough. The guy nodded and stood to one side.

Finally, he was next in the queue. He quickly explained to the pretty girl the other side of the desk. She directed him to the Help Desk which was situated on the opposite side of the departure lounge. Luckily there was no queue and no one waiting. By the time Billy had run as fast as he could back, another glamorous lady had already been informed by the one on the booking in desk. She greeted him with a big cheesy grim, 'At last we have found you sir, we have been expecting you to show up.'

The passports and flight tickets had been handed in three weeks ago, when someone found them left on the suitcase trolley in the multi-story car park.

How could they have known they were flying back to the UK on a British Airways flight? Now all was well and once again they boarded another flight by the skin of their teeth.

The carrier bag still had the colouring books inside, as well as the crayons much to the delight of the children. Ronda was a bit miffed they had stolen her perfume. But she was just thankful their plight was over.

Billy had suggested they had taken the perfume as a thank you payment for doing the right thing.

'Don't worry darling,' he told his wife, 'I will buy you another bottle of perfume, the rest would have been far more costly,'

After such a long wait, they barely had time to say goodbye.

The family returned to Austria, the following year and the year that followed that, but they never flew, those times they DROVE!

# Chapter 4

## 'The Syndrome'
## 2000

Wednesday was a quiet day in the salon, only Ronda and Tracey worked that day.

It was freezing out; the sky was dark and heavy with snow. It was most unlikely anyone would venture out for the chance of a haircut. So the girls decided to do a stock check before placing the big Christmas product order.

While doing so, Ronda decided to give the store cupboard a good wipe down with the anti-bac. Back in the day, when the building was someone's home this would have been used as a pantry. Right at the back were some old tatty boxes used to store things the salon no longer needed. Ronda went rummaging to find an old 50`s style hairdryer, like the red one her mother used many moons ago. There was a unique pair of hand clippers, left by the barber who retired from the business before the salon was modernized in present day.

There was an odd object that looked as though they may have been used as crimpers in the 1920`s. The contents of the old boxes intrigued Ronda; it seemed a shame to part with them so she found herself justifying the keep when really, they needed the space for the new stock. It was always a struggle to find anything as nothing was laid out neatly and it did need a good thorough clean. To put these boxes back where they had been stored for what must have been decades, would be like putting back the dust and cobwebs. Ronda and Tracey decided between them they needed to go!

Then Ronda noticed something, it wasn't similar to anything she had seen before until she studied it more closely. It was a soft rubber ball, that had started to perish with age. Attached, was a nylon tube that looked like a fat piece of rope. On the end of that was a metal threaded end which looked as though it was meant to screw onto something. She put it aside while she looked inside the second box to see if she could find the gadget that seemed to be missing. At first nothing jumped out at her, but as she started to add things to the 'to be dumped' pile, she noticed a strange metal object that resembled a nozzle. It had a round opening at the top which looked as though it was waiting to be screwed to something. Hmm, she thought. She took the strange attachment to see if the two parts went together as one, and indeed they did. The metal ends were in need of an oil as they clearly hadn't been used in years. After a tiny blob of WHAL oil, generally used to keep the electric clippers in good working order, the two gadgets screwed nicely together, they were obviously an ancient historic hairdressing object, but what could it be used for? It reminded Ronda of the re-fillable perfume spray her mother had on her dressing table. But the pretty pink cut glass bottle had been re-placed with this larger rubber ball.

Could it have been used as a hair lacquer applicator, Ronda had a vague memory of her mother using one but they were always like a plastic squeezy bottle. Could it possibly be used for those years before her time?

Although Tracey was a good ten years Ronda's junior, she seemed to know exactly what the mystery gadget was used for, 'It`s an old powder puff, used to dust the client's neck after a cut.' In present day, a tiny bit of talc would be sprinkled on the neck brush before each use, it helped dust off the loose hair snippings that sometimes stuck to the client's skin, especially when wet. That figured, they used talc for other things in the salon too. Giving damp perm curlers a good dusting with talc after they had been rinsed help prevent the damp rubbers from perishing.

Ronda was like a child with a new toy, she decided they should put it to good use.

After a good soak in some hot water with Fairy washing up liquid, she gave it a gentle waft with the hair dryer, so the talc wouldn't clog together, and filled it up with some Johnsons baby powder, adding that to the stock list order. She was delighted how well it puffed out just the right amount and felt a tiny bit excited about using it.

Ronda's new gadget came into good use, Simon especially liked using it, then the one time it ran out of talc, (someone who never owned up, had filled it too full.) Ronda picked it up to use on her gent's neck and puff,' her gent disappeared into a cloud of talc as half its contents filled the poor chap's neck ole.

*'It could only happen to Ronda'*

It was a cold crispy day with sunshine. As Christmas vastly approached, Ronda was aware she needed to get her shopping in order. It would have already been bought and gift wrapped by November but it was now early December which left her feeling anxious and rushed.

Lizzie and Bella collected `Colour Box Teddy Bears,` The only place you could buy them in the small market town of Spalding was the family run business of J.T. Whites. This was the girls favourite place to spend their pocket money, but they were pretty pricey therefore they saved for several weeks before they could add to the collection. However, these joyful little bears made delightful stocking fillers, so after another exhausting day at the Salon, Ronda decided it would be one more thing crossed off the never-ending long list of things to do.

In spite of Ronda's chronic pain, she proceeded to walk the short distance to the china shop across the Sheep Market square. By the time she was opening the door that triggered a bell, Ronda felt crushed by profound fatigue.

This was one of the many symptoms of fibromyalgia syndrome diagnosis made earlier that year. Ronda was feeling more than crap as she persevered in taking her body to the highest level of pain she could tolerate. Determined not to allow it to get the better of her she had already made the decision to this small errand at the first light of day.

After a short browse and telling the lovely shop assistant what she had decided to buy, the chatty young lady asked, 'Would you like them gift wrapped?'

She thought for a moment or two before answering, 'Umm, yes, go on then, it will save me the job, thank you.'

Ronda watched the shop assistant gift wrap each one in turn, adding a gift tag with each daughter's name so they didn`t get mixed up. Once she had added the thin ribbon, she watched as the young lady curled the ribbon by running the blade of a thin pair of scissors along its edge, exactly how Ronda used to do at Hoppers.

'That`ll be, forty-two pounds and seventy-five pence, please.'

After Ronda had written the cheque and handed it over, the pretty young lady opened the till. She instantly smiled sweetly as she handed the cheque back to Ronda.

'What`s wrong?' Ronda queried seriously, while the young lady tried to brace a smile.

'What?' Ronda chided taking the cheque back in her right hand.

She looked puzzled she couldn't see any error on the cheque at all. She had signed and dated it and done everything perfectly, or so she thought.

'What's wrong with it?' she asked again.

The pretty young lady, pointed to the end of the line where Ronda had written forty-two pounds and seventy-five pence, please. The small error was as clear as day, but in spite of Ronda starring right at it, she couldn't seem to grasp the problem.

She even read it out loud, 'Forty-two pounds and

seventy-five pence, please.'

Ronda, stared wide eyed when the young lady by the name of Debbie pointed directly at the word, `PLEASE.`

Between the two of them they just laughed loudly!

Ronda instantly tore the cheque up, and took great care to write a second one. As she handed it back to Debbie who was standing on the opposite side of the counter, Debbie covered her mouth with the palm of her hand as she sniggered, 'Oh no,' she said. 'You've done it again.'

That was Ronda's last cheque and she had another errand to do before home.

By this time the pair of them were in hysterics with laughter, when the snooty older woman came out of the back room, (assuming the office) wearing a sour face and pursed lips, just how Mr. Jacobs used to.

Ronda had felt rather chastised as the older women's face tightened with indignation.

One of the joys about thought is no one knows what you are thinking about them. Sometimes thought gave powers words never could because they never cause a confrontation. Skills Ronda had learnt over the years with her own father who often had the same peevish look about him, that left the identical furrows across his forehead as though life was just one big headache.

This woman was above her station and Ronda knew she was only a mere minimum wage shop assistant. Ronda had grown up knowing the Hensel family and this woman wasn't one of them. Mr and Mrs Hensel, who had owned J.T Whites down the generations before them, were well to do folk, but not haughty like this woman was. Ronda had never been made to feel so belittled in this shop until now.

'What seems to be the problem madam?' she asked tersely.

'Nothing,' Ronda replied, thinking had she smiled only slightly she would have cracked her foundation, while she gave Debbie a wink, Ronda proceeded to tell the older lady with certitude 'It`s all under control, thank you.'

Ignoring Ronda as though she was completely invisible, she spoke to Debbie slowly with some agitation as though she was under suspicion like some halfwit.

Debbie replied politely to try and save any embarrassment, 'The lady made a small error on her cheque, if she crosses it out and initials it, would that be acceptable Mrs. Grey?' she asked graciously as though she had rehearsed it several times in her head.

'I have used my last cheque, you see,' Ronda explained in a light tone.

'Let me see,' Mrs Grey scoffed as she snatched the cheque from Debbie's hand.

'That's fine, it's perfectly fine as it is, I cannot understand why there`s such a melodrama over it.'

And the nasty old bag sniffed as she slammed the cheque through the till and walked off.

Leaving Ronda and Debbie chuckling between them.

'Do you think I should leave my number just in case she notices the error at the end of the day?' Ronda suggested.

'Well, on her head so be it, she has just put it through as her sale, so any commission goes to her.' Debbie chided. 'She's been doing that ever since I worked here, every chance she gets.'

'Oh, that has just made my day,' Ronda giggled. 'Is she always full of the jollies?' Ronda laughed again.

Ronda left the shop beaming a wide mouthed grin to herself. While she noticed others along the High Street returning the smile, Ronda wondered if only they knew!

'Oh, I do things like that all the time,' people would say, but for Ronda things just seemed to get worse. It was apparently all part of the syndrome.

Back at the car, Ronda used her fob to unlock the boot of her car to no avail. So she tried the door and still nothing. The fatigue drained through her every limb as her legs weakened, she felt them buckle in panic. She glanced around to see if anyone was watching.

Well, you feel so silly, don't you? Anyway, there wasn't any clear evidence that anyone was - 'watching,' so she tried several times again. Confused by each attempt as the fob light continued to flicker with each click.

With the delay at J.T. Whites with the cheque pantomime - due to Ronda being far too polite with her pleases, Ronda was already concerned about being late to meet Bella from school. But she had no choice but to walk to Wilkinson store as fast as her weary legs could carry her, to purchase a packet of fob batteries.

Back at the car she changed the fob battery but it still failed to unlock her car, by which time Ronda could have wept. As she was about to walk back to the salon to phone the school to warn Bella she would have to make her own way home from school, a handsome young gentlemen asked if she was, okay.

Once Ronda had explained he started with a giggle, 'Well it won't unlock the door sweetheart, that's my car.'

'So, if that's your car, where the dickens is mine?' Ronda gasped with a sigh, feeling a very big bit foolish.

'It shouldn't be too difficult to find if you aim the fob at all the silver Rovers in the car park,' he chided. 'Shall I help you look?' Ronda thanked him kindly and handed him the fob.

The fob light continued to flash so Ronda's car should have been in view, although there only seemed to be another two silver Rovers parked close enough for the light to flicker.

Poor Ronda tried so hard to contain herself as she remembered her face filled with an embarrassing heat as her cheeks turned scarlet. When she remembered she no longer owned a silver Rover, she had no choice but admit she was actually looking for the wrong car. Truth be told, she had been driving her new black Focus for the last three weeks and counting.

The chap went on his way, laughing to himself behind his steering wheel, so that was the second person who had a laugh at her expense that day.

*The joys and trepidations of Ronda . . .*

Ronda's shopping and car park nightmares never seemed to waver. Her confidence and self-esteem seemed to become more and more depleted with each fibromyalgia flare up.

On this occasion Ronda needed to return the library books. The short stay parking spaces directly outside the library was now a taxi only parking bay. So, Billy offered to drive his wife into the town and do a sit and wait in the car park, while Ronda ran in to return the books. He often did this when her legs pained her or the fatigue was getting the better of her.

When she returned to their black Ford Focus, she opened the door, sat beside her husband reading the newspaper and buckled up. 'Come on then, let's get going,'
'OK babe, where would you like to go?' answered the unfamiliar voice.

Her heart started to pulsate, she had not only sat in someone else's car but next to someone else's husband. He had allowed her to buckle up and at what point was he ever going to tell her? After he reversed out of the parking bay?

The older gentleman seemed to take it all in his stride, as he made a joke, 'I thought we were going on a bit of a date.'
'It's a good job you didn't drive off with me then,' she said noticing Billy glancing out of the driver's

window of the car parked alongside them.

Rushing to get out as quickly as she possibly could do, Ronda struggled. She leant forward but seemed restricted. She had already opened the door and swung her legs round, but seemed to be stuck rigid to the seat.

'Try unbuckling the safety belt love,' the old bloke chuckled.

She could not get out of the car quick enough, before she did anything else foolish but her heel caught in the safely strap as it dropped to the foot well, she toppled over flashing her under wear in the process.

Billy however, sat in bulls eye view watching all of this, by the time she sat at the side of him in the right car, he was beyond hysteria. He was literally crying real tears.

*As was the older gentlemen in the other black Ford Focus.*

# Chapter 5

## 'Fibro Fog'

If you are a mother, you may well have experienced 'Baby Brain,' but has any one of you ever experienced the Syndrome 'Fibro Fog?'

Well, this takes you to a higher level, it happens to you more than once a day, every single day until you start to believe you are going completely crackers. Ronda had never suffered in her life before her fibromyalgia diagnosis, and now she seemed to be getting everything the other way round, back to front or upside down. Her words mix up, her sentences, her spelling, everything you can think about. Even spell check does not recognise her spelling errors.

The fibromyalgia continued to haunt Ronda, it followed her around like a nasty sticky substance stuck to her joints.

It wasn't only chronic pain that plagued her, it was something in the atmosphere that weighed her down like heavy sand.

Ronda's central nervous system seemed to be wired up all wrong. Her brain was perceiving pain she did not have, as though she was injured badly but no physical damage could be seen. Only Ronda thought she had been in the boxing ring with Mike Tyson. On the outside she looked perfectly healthy, but she was in so much pain, she could barely stand on her feet all day. She had lost so much muscle strength in her arms she struggled to hold the hair dryer. Her fingers and hands cramped as they went into spasm. She dropped things, she cut her own self every single day with the sharp hair dressing scissors. Things slipped out of her hand and broke on the floor, she had a narrow escape when she dropped the hairdryer one day, luckily, she caught it just before it hit her client's head. Her co-ordination was all wrong, she lost her balance, she tripped easily, fell down the stairs, and if you didn't know she was a tea total type of girl, you would think she was in a drunken stupor!

Her migraines came in clusters, resulting in bed rest for the best part of a week. She wasn't even forty and had no idea how she was going to make it through the day. She felt like a little old lady with the onset of dementia. So while everyone found Ronda funny, she always felt like everyone else's bit of fun.

When this began, she had no idea, I suppose it crept on her gradually and she was so used to pushing herself, her life had become one challenge after another, it simply became normal for Ronda. Until . . .

The day came when she ceased to function at all. Her GP suspected multiple sclerosis, but the tests were negative. It soon became clear what wasn't wrong with Ronda, as each symptomatic condition was ruled out. The hard part was the not knowing what was wrong with her. Ronda felt as though she was a fraud, like an attention seeking weakling. Four years later a new rheumatologist came up with a diagnosis no one had heard of before. Fibromyalgia Syndrome. Broken down it means fibrous tissues 'fibro' - such as tendons and ligaments, muscles- 'my' and pain 'algia'. The syndrome part means a collection of other symptoms that seem to go hand in hand with the miserable rest of it.

Adding to that diagnosis, another consultant diagnosed her with CFS which stands for chronic fatigue syndrome, the syndrome partly over laps with many of the fibromyalgia symptoms. The two combined resulted in a progression of other symptoms such as cognitive impairment causing poor memory, dizziness, tingling sensations, neuropathy, sensitivity to hot weather, cold weather, blurred vision, chronic profound fatigue, severe migraine symptoms, walking difficulties, shaking, extreme sensitivity to stress, repetitive activity, any form of exercise, slight dyslexia brought on by fatigue. With this dire combination Ronda spent more time in bed than she did out of it.

As her plight continued, she tried to understand the dilemmas she had to deal with.

The harder she fought against life's challenges, the more she suffered for it. A good night's sleep made little difference, pacing, exercise and plenty of rest only seemed to add to her frustrations. She could rest and sleep for over a week and feel no better for it. In fact, she wasn't getting any better at all. Only worse . . .

When Ronda was a child growing up in the 60`s her mother often seemed to be frog marching her off to the doctor's surgery. They didn't have an appointment system back in the day. It was a sit and wait your turn system, by working out who was the person before you and who was the person after you.

She didn't seem to be plagued with the childhood ailments other children did, her mother would put her in bed with her brother to catch whatever it was that was being passed around the school playground. The only thing Ronda can ever recall catching was the chicken pox. Other than that, it was either growing pains or tonsillitis and migraine from the age of eleven.

*I know what you might be thinking, `**hypochondriac!**`*

Ronda danced from the age of four years, until her sixteenth birthday. With every new dance routine, she complained about sore muscles. Her dance teacher said that meant she was giving it her all. But Ronda needed pain medication to get her to school the following days ahead. This only seemed to worsen with each birthday.

By the late 80`s Ronda joined a gym, she found it difficult but she could only give it her best.

By the 1990's she joined a Step Reebok class, which floored her.

After a total break of any form of exercise, she joined a Line Dancing Class which she loved. However, by the time the class had finished Ronda could barely walk or stand as her muscles froze in agonizing pain. She drove home in pain and by the time she was pulling on her drive her legs had totally ceased up, resulting in her physically lifting her legs by hand to get out of the car. There was no strength to pick them up to step into the front door. And the only way to bed was bumpety-bump one step of the stairs at a time.

As time passed, she had no idea how she was ever going to move forward from this. She looked drained and haggard, as she fell apart both physically and mentally. Everyone told her how well she looked, while inside she was breaking into pieces.

This was Ronda's secret hell. Her confidence dropped, her self-esteem became non-existent and the depression made her feel as though she was unworthy of the human race. And every morning she felt as though she had been crushed under a Mac-Truck.

Her GP suggested water exercise, so Ronda went swimming but after pushing herself to swim thirty lengths of the local swimming pool, which amounted to about a mile, Ronda needed the help of the dishy young life guard to heave her out of the water. When she stood her legs went to jelly and she had no strength to hold herself up.

Sometimes it took all her strength to shower and wash her hair, on a better day she was able to put her makeup on, and if she was having a much better day, she could probably manage to dry her hair. After swimming forget it, it would result in a short drive home and straight to bed for the rest of the day and the day after that, and the day after that sometimes too.

There were times she made it as far as the front door, but drive she could not. The times Billy would get as far as St John's Church and he would have to turn the car around in the gate entrance of the school, to take his wife back home.

Other times they would reach their destination but Ronda was too weak to get out of the car. She would sit in the car park while Billy went off to do the weekly super market shop, on his own.

And all Ronda wanted to do was CRY . . .

# Chapter 6

## 'A Big ASK – 2000'

Ronda searched for a new purpose in her life, something other than a wife, a mother and a hairdresser - she wanted to do something new and exciting and she had this great need to help others. But with such ill health was she even capable? She had no idea what value she could be to others anyway.

At this time in Ronda's life, she had been asked by her pain clinic consultant if she was interested in running a support group at the hospital. They would refer the patients to the group and support Ronda in any way they could do. She was not only flattered but she knew this could help her too.

Ronda had studied her illness from the first day of her diagnosis, she had read lots of on-line information and read many books on the subject, in her findings she saw her own reflection in the many debilitating symptoms.

She was already an active member of the Fibromyalgia Association UK, who had been tremendously helpful. So much so, Ronda was already manning the national help lines as a part time volunteer. Ronda attended one or two meetings with the pain clinic management team and the decision was made on the grounds Ronda could cope with it, and pace herself without making her own symptoms worse.

At first the group consisted of a few patients from the

NHS pain management clinic. The hospital supplied a vacant room with tables and chairs, the rest was left to Ronda. She felt as though she had so much to give, so each month she set out a meeting plan and updated the pain clinic team so they were fully aware of how things were progressing.

The support met the first Monday in every month from 11.00am to 2.00pm. The group continued to grow when Ronda noticed that many of these patients had also been diagnosed with chronic fatigue syndrome which was the once M.E (Myalgia encephalitis) diagnosis. The medical profession started to pooh pooh the M.E diagnosis and some physicians out ruled it altogether saying that *encephalitis* was not present in those who had been diagnosed with M.E. Although this serious condition may start with flu-like symptoms very much like those who had been diagnosed with 'Yuppy Flu' it made head line news in News of the World, until everyone began to believe M.E. didn't exist at all. What the social media failed to mention was the fact these symptoms were very real; they had just been given the wrong label.

The term M.E soon held a stigma against its diagnosis and all sorts of stories went flying around. The sufferers were soon labelled as malingerers, hypochondriacs and time wasters until they were not given very much loyalty at all.

No one even took their symptoms seriously; some were told to find a change in employment; they were sent for psychotherapy; they were put on anti-depressants; while their symptoms escalated out of control.

Their families and friends turned their back on them, no one was giving them the time of day. It simply became a bad word and its new stigma became the new 'Yuppy Flu' and that label served its ignorance too, as most people believed that it only affected young students who were burning their candle at both ends while away from home at university.

This added to a lot of the stress and frustration, the patients were told to do the utmost ridiculous things, exercise being one of a few.

Ronda made notes from everyone's story and reviewed them, a pattern soon emerged, they all had a lot of things in common with one another.

But why the cognitive behavior therapy suggestions known in short as CBT? Why the anti-depressants? Ronda studied that too and found a plan to convince the patients that the prescribed drugs did not mean they were depressed although most of the sufferers suffered from that too.

After six months the pain clinic had noticed a huge difference in patients' attitudes, while receiving an awful lot of positive feedback, they seemed to be managing their condition much better. Not something the clinic alone had been able to achieve.

Sadly, with every group there will always be one who shows signs of negativity, not everyone liked Ronda for a variety of reasons. Ronda had hidden her own symptoms a great deal in the hope the patients would soon try to help themselves a little more. They were all made aware that Ronda was also a patient, but a few overlooked that fact and expected more than she was capable of giving.

Ronda had permission from the pain management team to write and publish a groups monthly newsletter, basically to go over the previous meeting, so anyone who had missed out could catch up. At first the pain clinic funded the newsletter which soon became more like a monthly magazine. Ronda designed a cover, she gave it contents, and tried to make it enjoyable rather than just full of the depressing stuff.

Originally the pain clinic agreed to fund the group and provide the venue for six months with an understanding, it would be reviewed after that time.

However, the group continued to be a success for over 2 years. Then suddenly with no warning the new extension in the outpatient department of the hospital meant that the support group room would be under construction, and the clinic had no other available space putting the group at risk of closure.

With a gutsy determination to fight for their self-help group Ronda, decided to keep the group running and this was when Pilgrim Support Group became independent.

Venues were expensive and this added to Ronda's concerns. Eventually, Ronda found a free venue at the *Health Care Clinic* in Spalding town.

She worked out a yearly subscription for the monthly

newsletter so the group would become self-funded. There would be no member fee to join the group, and it would be open to the 'general public' with the fibromyalgia/ chronic fatigue diagnosis.

The group needed advertising in order to branch out with the intention to offer more support.

Ronda, applied for group funding, she wrote to local charities such as the Spalding Round Table, Spalding Lions, and the group was awarded two National Lottery grants over a ten-year period, which enabled the group to update essential office equipment.

Over a period of time the members dwindled because they were travelling too far to the new venue, so Ronda searched for a second venue closer to the hospital. All was well as the group expanded. Working alongside Fibromyalgia UK, other group leaders around the UK, got to know one another quite well by name. There were opportunities to attend seminars, with each group funding their own expenses to attend, or pay for it out of their own pocket.

Ronda worked without complaint, sometimes from her own bed. Billy, rigged up an office in the corner of her bedroom so she could work until she needed rest and at times she crawled on her hands and knees from office chair to bed. She slept a good part of the day, sometimes for days at a time. Then she would struggle back to her desk to continue writing the monthly news. Now, they had lost the support from the hospital, each newsletter was published, printed and posted by Ronda.

She manned the help lines, more often than not, from her sick bed, working as a volunteer for The Fibromyalgia Association UK, alongside their advertised local group.

Ronda was good at this voluntary work, although she soon became more aware how easy some of the support work actually came to her. Ronda always seemed to have the right words for people even though she had not always shared the same experiences. I mean how do you talk a stranger out of suicide over the telephone? Well, in many ways it's easier when the other person is a stranger, and the listener/counsellor has no face to the voice. But Ronda never failed in finding the right words as they naturally flowed from her lips.

She often described it as though another person was speaking through her or taking the pen out of her hand as she wrote to people. Sometimes a long call could go on for two hours or more but each time Ronda was never the one to terminate the call. That was never part of her protocol.

These calls often left no memory of the conversations that had taken place, it was almost as though she was living inside a bubble in another world.

Ronda soon learned that with any group or charity there will always be the workers and always be the sitters. Then of course Rome wasn't built in a day. Ronda welcomed constructive criticism; it was the only way she would improve her support. All of this was a huge learning curve for Ronda and mostly she found her path as she went along and learnt by her own mistakes or feedback from the group members.

Ronda was feeling a spiritual connection but it wasn't clear or defined enough to explain. Then she felt a calling to visit 'Little Acorns,' at the Mousse Hall down Love Lane. She received healing and was told she had a white Angel as her guide.

*'You need to work at a slower pace, you need to start looking closer to home at your own health, you will have a few problems in the reproductive area, you will be ok but you must get things checked out at the hospital.'*

# Chapter 7

## 'You may well Laugh'
## 2008

The following Spring, Ronda took herself on a shopping spree, the weather was changing quickly, the worst of the winter months over, and the fashion shops had long finished the winter sales. Like most people Ronda was getting tired of wearing the bulky sweaters under her winter coat. She needed light weight jackets, cooler tops and some shoes to replace her fur lined boots.

The warmer weather gave her a sudden urge to treat herself. She had a wonderful alone time, wandering from shop to shop in the town centre. She was delighted with her purchases and just needed to go to Hills department store, for some suitable fabric to make cushion covers, for the new sofas they had ordered.

Ronda's cousin had worked in Hills from the day she left school. As it happened, she worked on the fabric counter.

She decided to go home to have a nice cup of tea before meeting the girls from school.

By the time Ronda pulled on her drive she was deflated by fatigue, which plagued her more often than not. The shopping trip had floored Ronda. Laden with heavy bags that dragged on her fibrous shoulders added to her already severe neck and back pain. She really should not have struggled to the department store for fabric they didn't have.

Ronda's feet were swollen and sore from the warm day and fur lined boots. She never did find a nice pair of shoes that would make do before it really was sandal weather.

On the brink of collapse, Ronda noticed the time, and decided the fifteen minutes she had spare before leaving the house to meet the girls from school was not long enough to have a much-needed cup of tea. She settled for a cold drink from the fridge, which to be fair cooled her down more than a hot drink could have done.

By the time Ronda was home again with the girls, panic leered over her, as she stood staring inside the empty boot of her car.

*'Where was her shopping?'*

She couldn't remember taking the bags into the house when she came home from the shops. Ronda searched in the most likely of places where she would have dumped the shopping. It was not in the entrance hall, it was not in the kitchen and it was not in her bedroom.

After checking the boot again and the back seats, Ronda started to shake, she had just spent over a hundred pounds and lost the bloody lot!

*'How could that possibly happen without her noticing?'*

Trying to think, Ronda started to back track where she had been. Starting with the last shop, Hills department store. Ronda gave them a call and asked to speak to her cousin, who said she would have a good look for her and call her back. But nothing had been found and no one else had noticed any suspicious Dorothy Perkins and New Look carrier bags.

Ronda was certain she had the shopping when she went in the department store because she remembered the pain carrying them from one end of the town to the other. However, she didn't appear to have missed them when she left the store. With Ronda anything was possible. She gave New Look a call, then Dorothy Perkins. No one had noticed any bags left in the changing rooms or on the shop floor and nobody had handed anything in.

Two days later Ronda's cousin gave her another call, she was delighted to tell Ronda her lost property had been found safely wedged in between several layers of curtaining fabric.

. . . .

A week or two later, everyone was excited about Bella getting married, Ronda and Bella had planned to visit Lizzie for lunch after another bridal fitting.

Bella`s two-bedroom end terrace came with a private car park to the rear of the property. Ronda was early, Ronda was always early, Bella was running late, Bella was always running late. Ronda parked in the available parking bay which had been allocated to Bella`s house number. They were given two parking bays to each house; this was fine because Chris had long left to work on the opposite side of town.

The front door of the house was open and there was a distant calling for the cat, who Bella was trying to coax towards the open door with a piece of cat nip. Once Tiger was safely inside the house, it left exactly five minutes to get to the bridal shop, and Bella was nowhere near ready. Frustrations ran high and left a lot of disagreements between Ronda and her daughter, which wasn't helped by Bella criticizing her mother's driving skills.

The dress fitting wasn't the most joyous occasion one would expect. Ronda was very emotional as soon as Bella tried on the first dress. Her baby, a bride and she looked so beautiful, she would have made any mother of the bride cry . . .

Eight dresses later - still counting and Ronda's tears were now for a very different reason, she was crushed by profound fatigue and pain.

'Oh no, where did I put it?' Bella muttered out loud while she rummaged through her handbag.

'Can you drive home first Mum? I must have left the C.D on the kitchen table.

'Well really Bella,' her mother scoffed. 'Is it important? Only we are already running an hour behind.'

'Yes, of course it's important, I want you to listen to it.'

'Another time might be better? My head is so painful, darling,'

Ronda's daughter thought not, this was the music she had chosen to walk down the aisle to. Bella had the afternoon planned and if this swung her, she`d be in a fluster for the rest of the day.

Just at that very second when Ronda indicated to turn into Hawthorn Bank, she somehow managed to stall the car on the T junction of St Johns Road.

Remembering this is a Ford Focus, one of the easiest cars on the road to drive, here they sat in the middle of a busy junction at one of the busiest times of the day, with every other set of wheels belonging to cars, trucks, lorries or vans, left to tediously manoeuvre around Ronda who was obstructing the road.

She was hooted at, ranted at, fisted at, even laughed at, but all she was capable of doing at that very moment in time was, sit and stare in a trance, with a blank expression. Bella`s voice was muffled and undefined.

'Mum, what are you doing?'

'I don`t know what to do,' Ronda triple stammered with panic.

'Try putting your hand break on would be a good start,' her daughter scoffed.

'Now, neutral, turn the engine on and first gear,' she chided.

The gears crunched while she hit the gas instead of the clutch.

'Mum, stop mucking about, seriously, you are going to be the cause of an accident if you don`t pull yourself together.'

Truth be told, Ronda was not messing, she had literally forgotten how to drive!

'Okay, deep breath, first gear, hand break off, now mirror, signal, manoeuvre,'

'I'm okay, I'm just so tired.'

'All the more reason why I should drive to Bourne,' Bella chided with attitude.

'No, you can't, the car is not insured for you to drive,' her mother insisted.

'That's as maybe Mum, but I think it would be the safer option, otherwise tomorrow's news will be about mother and daughter killed in road traffic accident three yards from their drive way.'

Panicking, Ronda left the engine running while she unfastened her seat belt, opened the car door and climbed out to change places with her daughter. While Bella drove the short distance down the Park Way to Horseshoe Road.

Back on Bella's car park, she stood outside the car door, waiting for her mother as she observed her rocking forward and back in a rhythm like a child on a rocking horse. But Bella couldn't quite relate to the meaning of her mother's strange behaviour.

'What the fuck, is wrong with you Mother?'

'I'm stuck Bella, I can't get out of the car seat.'

'Well, maybe you would if you tried unlocking the safety belt,' Bella scoffed without humour.

The only response Ronda received that day from her daughter was sheer utter annoyance. There was no empathy or concern for her actual wellbeing AT ALL!

Before Bella had driven out of the car park in her own

car, she was playing the CD.

Ronda sobbed and sobbed like a lost whale at sea, as the music played out loudly.

'You can`t Bella, you can`t do this to me, I am going to be in such a state and my mascara will be running before the service even begins.'

'You will be fine, Mother. Just play it over and over again until it no longer makes you feel emotional,' she patronized.

By the time they arrived at Lizzie's, their mother not only pitched up with a strained, puffy face, the red swelling around her tearful eyes, spoke a thousand words.

'What's up with `er?' Lizzie asked after one glance at their mother.

'Don`t ask,' Bella chuckled with a smirk and a shake of the head.

But the day was far from over - when Bella drove her mother back to Spalding to pick up her own car from Bella's car park, she watched her mother unlock the passenger door, sit in the passenger seat and buckle up.

Bella tapped on the window . . .

*'Mum, who the fuck is going to drive you home?'*

# Chapter 8

## 'Ronda's Story'

**So, how did it all start for me?** How did I know? Well truth be told the first time I had no idea at all.

Ovarian Cancer had always been the biggest fear in my life, worse than drowning, worse than burning. I feared never seeing my children grow up, I feared never seeing my girls marry, being part of my grandchildren's life, or ever writing the book I was determined to do one day.

A lot of people may think I am materialistic, I am the opposite: none of those things really matter to me. Love and happiness always come first. But hay ho, it doesn't matter how much money you make, it won`t change the outcome.

Living long enough to fulfil my needs and leaving this world before I grow old and haggard, then I could not wish for anything better.

I am sixteen years older than my mum now, she passed away on her forty seventh birthday. I celebrated my sixty third this year, which I didn't think I would ever do from my prognosis in the year 2010. So, after a long eight years remission the cancer had returned, but in 2021 I am still here, I guess miracles can happen sometimes.

My mum will always be remembered forever young,

so will several of my very dear friends. Whatever age we are there will always be unfinished business and I will always think of something else I'd like to achieve. But the scariest thing for me now is, the speed that time travels. Eleven years since my first cancer diagnosis - gone far too quickly.

I was forty years old when the fibromyalgia hit me at its worse, I did everything in my power to get better. I had several sessions of holistic treatment, two practitioners told me they could pick something up in my pelvis area and told me to get checked out. Around about that time my father was nagging me to have a scan. That's easier said than done, it's convincing your GP that you need a scan, and too many scans can cause cancer, so it begins to feel like a no-win situation.

'Beat Cancer Early' they say, words that are far harder than you can possibly imagine. Unless you have damage to your DNA that puts your risk higher than Mr. or Mrs. average, you won't be entitled to regular scans at a young age. One known relative from my maternal blood line didn't put me in a high-risk category to be tested for the faulty BRCA gene, however my GP did honour a scan, and it was clear. What more could I do to protect myself from this deadly fear that I continued to carry around with me? Day in, day out it dragged me down further as the weight on my shoulders became a huge burden to bear.

The only thing to do now was to be body aware and vigilant to anything untoward. Apart from the debilitating fibromyalgia and chronic fatigue I tested healthy.

It was a couple of months before my fifty second birthday when I started to have women's problems.

I had none of the ovarian cancer symptoms but I knew something was odd. I was having huge gaps between my periods, then for no reason or warning I would have a flash flood of bright red blood. There was no warning pain, in fact no pain at all. But it was a concern, once I had sorted myself out in the bathroom, there wasn't even spotting or discharge, not before, not after, it was just a gush and that'd be it.

The day Billy`s father was blue lighted to A & E with a suspected stroke, Billy and myself followed the ambulance with Billy`s mum taking a back seat. We had no need to rush, we would most probably have a long wait once we reached the hospital. So, Billy drove with caution as the flashing blue light sped ahead until it faded out of view.

The three of us waited in the family waiting bay until Billy`s mum needed a pee. She had left her walker at home so I, escorted her with linked arms to the toilets. She wasn`t happy about locking the doors, so I stood on the other side keeping guard. Suddenly with no warning I felt a warm sensation between my thighs. There was no pain, there never was but it usually happened after making love. Trying not to look too conspicuous, I leaned forward slightly to take a peek.

OH MY GOD! A massive patch of bright red blood covered the crutch of my thin white linen crop pants. Holy Cow! Without even thinking about knocking, I quickly opened the bathroom door, banged it closed, and locked it without hesitation.

A bewildered mother-in-law stared agog while sat on the toilet. We couldn`t make it up, could We?

All I could do was panic, while I lifted my long shirt to show my mum-in-law what all the faff was about, without uttering a single word, a sympathetic 'Oh no,' passed her lips while she stared wide eyed at her daughter-in-law`s crutch.

'What am I going to do?' I choked.

And from that moment Billy's mum kind of became my mum and I was so glad she was there.

The first time I thought I was having a period; the second time I suppose I thought the same. Thereafter I just wondered if it was the menopause. I had no mum to ask but my mother-in-law gave me a couple of stories about when it happened to her during the onset of her menopause. But I still made an appointment to see my GP because I thought this was maybe how it started with my own mum too. I had a vague memory that her symptoms, whatever they were, were blamed onto the menopause.

The GP didn`t seem unduly worried but she was fully aware of my family history and my worst fears, so she said she would refer me for a scan.

The weeks went by, I heard nothing, the weeks ran into months and still I had heard nothing, so I decided to chase things up with my GP, who told me. I had been referred and they had to honour the appointment before 16 weeks from the referral date. It had been twelve weeks by this time.

I was not happy to wait another four weeks, so she advised me to call the hospital to check things were in place. She said that they would take more notice of the patient, than of the doctor! Looking back on all that now, that was very wrong, no patient should do the doctor's donkey work, usually hospitals consultants take notice of GPs and vice versa.

I gave the hospital a call, they had no referral, I hadn't even been added to the waiting list and they couldn't add me without the G. P`s authorization. So I called the doctor back, of course I wasn't able to speak with her, it went through the receptionist to the GP, then back to me.

The GP insisted the hospital had received the referral and they insisted they hadn't and disagreeing was wasting too much time for me.

Use my experience as a learning curve for all of you women of a certain age, at any age . . . because many people would have taken the doctor's word for it and continued to wait. In spite of my then - GP insisting her referral had been sent to the hospital, the hospital still claimed, they had not received it. They must have done; it went through internal mail. Something was clearly very wrong with the system.

Anyway, putting that to one side I asked my GP if she could send a second referral, she did but the hospital claimed they hadn't received that one either and this went on several times before they finally did get the referral. By this time I had lost faith in both hospital and GP. Twelve weeks had already been wasted to no avail and I was still at the bottom of the waiting list, even though this second request should have been an urgent one.

I experienced a nagging feeling in my head that I must put myself in charge. The only thing to do now was request a second referral to an out of county hospital and request it as an emergency. At least then I would be seen quicker than twelve to sixteen weeks. Luckily, my G.P did honour that request, and within two weeks an appointment came through for an ultra sound scan at the out of county City Hospital of Peterborough, in Cambridgeshire.

I had no idea from that moment in time an avalanche of events would quickly follow, turning my whole world upside down and inside out. It's when one thing goes bad and other things follow.

# Chapter 9

## '1995 – 2010'

Audrey Cooper and Fairy paused their gossiping as Ronda Stone came tripping along Stonegate, her high heels tapped out a staccato message, 'Look at me, look at me,' and so they stared, hating her beauty with her perfectly applied lipstick which complimented her hazel eyes.

'I wonder where she`s off, all glammed to the nines?' Audrey queried accusingly as she wiped the dried pink windowlene off the window.

As Ronda glided past gracefully, 'Stuck up Bitch,' Audrey uttered under her breath.

'Say it loud enough, so I can hear you,' Ronda said in a humorous tone.

She wasn`t going to lower herself to their level just because they had no charisma and chose to wear cross over pinnies and knotted turbans to cover their rollers.

'Anyone would think `er old man was loaded, she finks she`s too grand to live round `ere,' Fairy seethed.

'Er old man might be loaded, but only cause `es as tight as a monkey's balls.'

'Talk says she`s knocking some posh tosh off on the new estate, the other side of town.'

'I know who `ya mean, but `ave ya seen `im? I can`t imagine someone messing around wiff the likes of `im.'

'Know what ya mean, fink she knows when `er

bread's buttered on the right side, I like `er bloke, `e's a really nice chap, kind and steady.'

Ronda was aware how that generation of folk liked to gossip while their windowlene dried. But she also knew that if they weren`t gossiping about her, they would be about someone else. Ronda's dignity did not mean she was playing around, however she was hiding something, something even too deep to discuss with her Billy . . .

It was FEAR . . .

*Fear from what no one dare mention, but Ronda knew if she didn`t speak of it soon, she`d be up shit street without a paddle.*

. . . .

Ronda was singing as she rinsed the soap bubbles from her aching limbs under the warm shower.

It was a pamper morning, she had shaved her legs and applied a face mask, she had no idea why! Her bikini line had been newly waxed and her plucked eyebrows made her feel clean and flawless, but she had no inclination to believe she was far from flawless on the inside.

She applied her make-up quickly, and after a quick blast with the hair dryer she carefully selected a dress from the wardrobe. It was a good choice, maybe she thought it would offer her a tiny bit of dignity while she spread her legs to do whatever was necessary.

The devoted couple had a good run to the hospital. They had missed the morning traffic and school time rush. They arrived twenty minutes early for the appointment.

It took no time at all to find a disabled parking space, right outside the main entrance to the out-patients. They displayed the ticket that Ronda had been recently awarded due to the progression of her fibromyalgia, which has to be said, was more of a concern than that day's appointment. She was only here because of the constant nagging in her own head, not to mention the ongoing spiritual messages each medium gave her. She was still convinced the bleeding was un-related.

Once they had reported their arrival with the very nice receptionist who warned them the radiographer was running late, they headed towards the coffee machine for their first coffee of the day. Billy needed a tipple of brandy to settle his stomach ache, as his belly churned into hundreds of tiny knots.

'I don`t know why you`re in such a state,' Ronda chuckled, 'It`s me who`s going to be poked and prodded with a big fat dildo.'

'Uh!'

'Oh, never mind, I`ll have a muffin with my latte.'

'How can you eat at a time like this,' her husband chided.

'Well, us women get used to these things, anyway it`ll all be a waste of bloody time, no need sweating the small stuff, until it turns into big stuff, eh!'

Ronda seemed to take it all in her stride. Besides, she

needed to keep a level head if she wanted the gynecologist to take her seriously, otherwise today's appointment would all be in vain!

The hospital was in chaos, as it was in the midst of a big move over to the brand-new Peterborough City hospital the other side of town. Ambulances queued at the main entrance, while patients waited in line on their trolley beds. By next week the bulldozers would be pulling down the old Edith Cavell hospital.

The thirty-five-minute wait seemed longer - by the time her name was called out by the nurse, Ronda`s mind had gone totally blank.

She was taken into a small room with no day light, the bright light shone from the florescent light that hung above. The nurse offered her a pick of the chairs, while Billy stayed in the waiting zone.

With a sense of déjà vu, the same questions as her GP had asked were posed to Ronda:

1) Last date of period? - 'Don`t know'
2) Any bleeding in between? - 'Yes'
3) Any pain or discomfort? - 'No'
4) Swelling, bloating in the tummy area? - 'No'
5) Need to pee more often? - 'No'
6) Constipation? - 'No'
7) Digestive problems? - 'No'
8) Hot flashes, night sweats? - 'Yes'
9) Are you sexually active? -'What's it got to do with you?'
10) Could you be pregnant? - 'No'

As the nurse excused herself while she disappeared to have a chat with the consultant, Ronda sat waiting. The walls that divided the two rooms were so thin, they may as well have been chatting in the same room. What about confidential protocol, if she could hear them discussing her, then surely other patients might be able to.

The nurse returned to introduce her to the grumpy old beggar who she could hear in the next room. God he was loud. Ronda wanted to hush him, tell him others could hear all her private business. He scowled across his brow, he was rude, abrupt, arrogant and he certainly had no skills in his bedside manner AT ALL!

He asked the same ten questions again and Ronda answered more or less the same as before. . . `Don`t know, Yes, No, No, No, No, No, Yes, None of your business, No.'

'May I ask Mrs. Stone, why has your GP referred you here today?'

'For peace of mind.'

'Now, why would she do that?'

'Because my mother died from Ovarian Cancer at the age of forty-seven and I am now fifty-two,' she told him with a lump in her throat as the words lay heavy as she spoke them and remembered . . .

'What were her symptoms?'

'I don`t really know, just that her doctor had been telling her for years that it was the early menopause.'

'Well, you have no obvious signs that you need to be concerned other than a psychological one'

'But' . . . . . .

'Let me finish,' he scoffed with his hand in the air to silence her. 'As your GP has requested that we do an ultra sound scan, I have to follow it through, bearing in mind this is a total waste of the Trust's time and money.'

Ronda was fair in not liking his attitude, he made her feel belittled and stupid especially when he added . . . 'At least you can leave this hospital, go home for a nice cup of tea and peace of mind!

'Then what happens?' she asked.

'Nothing, I will NOT need to see you again.'

Well, that told her, but this time it was Ronda who raised her hand in the air and told him 'Wait, I`m not finished.'

'Yes', he said with an annoyance in his tone.

'OK, so when you find nothing sinister from the scan, can I ask you to put me on the waiting list for surgery?'

'My dear, radical operations like this cannot be taken lightly, no surgeon on this universe would take out healthy organs on a whim.'

'Then I will go private.'

'It makes no difference whether you are an NHS patient or a private patient, women do die on the operating table having such types of surgeries, you know.'

Ronda, did not believe him.

'So, can I have regular screening then?'

'Dear God, imagine if we agreed to do that for everyone, the whole NHS system wouldn't cope, my dear.'

She wished he would stop referring her as his dear, it felt patronizing if that's the right word.

Ronda, could hardly tell him about the spiritual warnings . . . But the nagging sense that something just didn't feel right, felt important.

Ronda was led into another small clinical room that offered no comforts other than the one chair. The nurse offered her a hospital gown to change into, and she waited to be taken into the scanning room. The treatment bed offered comfort, with several crisp white fluffed up pillows, a roll of fresh clean paper protected the mattress, there was even a little foot step to make it easier for patients with short legs.

As Ronda lay in an undignified position, the number of students observing made her feel anxious, although they weren't able to see anything private apart from the picture of her innards on the monitor screen.

The nurse who stood at her side offered her hand for comfort; Ronda pulled away in rejection. The silence was eerie and it made Ronda feel even more uncomfortable.

'I like your handbag,' the nurse said.

'Thanks,' were the only words Ronda was capable of saying.

'What are your plans when you leave the hospital today?' The nurse asked.

Ronda thought she was trying to distract her from what everyone else was interested in on the scanning machine screen.

No one spoke, Ronda found the only way to deal with this was through humour, 'My husband is treating me to lunch.' she replied. 'Oh, that's nice, where are you going?'

'McDonalds' she told her. Then everyone chuckled.

'I love McDonald's,' a nurse told the rest of the team.

'Me too' said another.

'We have one right opposite our house, which is rather a little too tempting after a twelve hour shift.

The radiographer did not seem amused, he snapped at his team asking them to pay attention to detail. 'Look at this' he told them. The room went still and silent as everyone stared with grim faces.

Ronda lifted her head from the pillows to gain a better look. She laughed, 'It looks like the flipping Grim Reaper' she chuckled. No one shared her sense of humour.

The probe inside her changed position, while the radiographer explained they were now zooming in to her cervix which, according to him, was a nice healthy shade of pink with no sign of cysts or erosion. He then switched the monitor off, and proceeded to examine her tummy, paying a lot more attention to her left side than her right. He asked if she was tender, but she didn`t feel anything only the pressure from his warm hands.

'What are your plans for this afternoon?' he asked.

'What you mean after my Big Mac and chips?'

'Would it be possible, to grab your lunch in the hospital? Because, I would like you to have an emergency CT scan before you go home today.'

'Why?' Ronda asked.

'Regrettably, I will be performing your hysterectomy after all, but I may need to refer you to Addenbrookes hospital in Cambridge - the CT scan should confirm that.'

Ronda nodded without asking any questions. She hadn't really processed what he was saying. All she could think was 'Great, he changes his bloody mind after he has already told me I could die from such an operation.'

'While you dress, the nurse will write out a blood test form and arrange that immediately, the results should be ready within the hour.'

By the time she joined Billy in the waiting zone she was too crushed to speak.

Immediately Billy could detect the emotion building up within his wife's eyes. He started to panic when he looked at the blood form she was crushing in her hand. The nurse pointed her in the direction of oncology for the blood test, Ronda was clueless, oncology was the cancer clinic. The nurse explained the blood test was needed to test the protein levels in her blood, she explained thirty-five and below was classed as a normal reading, although that can vary from one patient to another. Ronda was also unaware this blood test - CA 125 they called it, was a marker test used for ovarian cancer.

In the meantime, she was sent to the third floor to have a cannula fitted for the dye they wanted to run through her veins to give an extra clear photograph of her insides.

The nurse asked if she was ok with needles, 'Of course,' Ronda said, 'I'm not five.' The nurse liked her sense of humour.

'Short sharp scratch,' and it was all done.

The CT scan had been booked for two thirty that afternoon, which left them ninety minutes to lose. The time dragged and dragged, 'We could have gone for our Big Mac after all,' Billy thought, as he looked at his watch for the umpteenth time over the last thirty minutes.

The nurse, asked for a quiet word - so she took Ronda and her husband to one side to inform them her blood test reading was 1,080 . . .

At exactly two fifteen Billy and Ronda made their way to the fourth floor . . . 'Forth Floor - Doors opening.'

Following the sign post down the long corridor, turning left, then right and left again they entered a small waiting area. Billy was very quiet, he looked grey with worry. Ronda wasn't making much noise either. She just felt numb in speech as well as in thought.

A middle-aged lady around Ronda's age waited with her daughter who couldn't have been older than late teens. A pretty girl with long blonde hair and rosebud lips that smiled sweetly at her mother.

She suddenly removed a wig, exposing her hairless head leaving the long-curved scar visible for all to see. Her mother gripped her hand tightly to comfort her, as they waited in silence. Ronda and Billy welled up with watery eyes.

Then they were startled by a weak pitiful cry, that seemed to be closing in on them.

The hospital porter entered where they were seated with a frail elderly lady who lay on her hospital bed. She had obviously been brought down from one of the wards.

Her voice was faint and vague at first, but as she came closer you could identify her words. 'Please, please, please,' she begged, 'help me, help me,' she repeated over and over.

It was too much for Billy, he stood and legged it along the corridor until he was out of view, leaving Ronda with one single tear that rolled gently down her cheek.

By the time Ronda was called through to the scanner, she was feeling desperately sad. She noticed a nurse run from one of the scanning rooms to the ladies toilet, she seemed to be in floods of tears. This seemed to be affecting everyone.

As the scanner moved over Ronda's still body, she relaxed and enjoyed the comfort of the super soft mattress and selection of comfy pillows beneath her as the scanner instructed - 'Deep breath in - and hold - Breathe normally.'

The scanning machine moved a little further towards her chest, as it settled it revved its engine, then seemed to sigh.

'Deep breath in - and hold - Breathe normally.'

The scanner moved a little further along before it began to move slowly back down towards her pelvic.

'You ok Ronda?' the voice asked.

'Yes, thank you,' she answered with a sniffle.

'Just putting the dye through, now,'

The machine made a bit of a clanking noise before it huffed and puffed and revved some more. Then she felt it, the warm sensation from the dye that ran through her veins to her throat, it stayed there for a second as it burned like fire, it moved a little further down her body until it reached her pubic region, where it stopped and stung with the heat.

The machine spoke again, 'Deep breathe in - and

hold - Breath normally.'

'Deep breath in - and hold - Breathe normally.' As the engine from the scanner slowly died, the nurse announced, 'ALL DONE!'

By the time Ronda had waited in recovery and had her cannula removed Billy was back in the waiting area.

It had been a harrowing day, and now it was time to go home. Neither of them spoke a single word until they were seated and buckled in the car, then Ronda let it all out as the tears fell, she hiccoughed and howled like a child in pain. Billy leaned over and hugged her. 'I thought you had been coping a little too well,' he said.

I just can`t stop thinking about that lady crying 'Help me!' That was typical of Ronda always thinking of someone going through something much worse than she was.

Six days later, as Ronda sang to the radio and danced around the kitchen while licking the cake mixture out of the mixing bowl that had once belonged to her mother, the telephone startled her, she turned the radio down and spoke in a jolly tone, 'Hello 724110, Ronda speaking.'

'Hello, can I please speak to Mrs. Ronda Stone?' the voice spoke seriously.

'Speaking,' Ronda replied.

'Hello Ronda, this is Peterborough City Hospital here, we have studied your scan results and had an MDT (multi-disciplinary team) meeting today, an appointment has been made for you tomorrow with the consultant Mr. Gloom at Addenbrookes hospital tomorrow afternoon, would you be able to be there?'

As she spoke the words would not flow, a feeble 'Yes' was all she could manage.

Deep down she knew what this meant but she could not bring herself to spit the words out to ask any questions. Part of her didn't want to know, she had spent the past three decades worrying about it and now it was happening for real it was just too much to bear. She wanted to run, run and hide from the reality of all this ugly business.

Billy, what about Billy? She must call him to make sure he can get time off to drive her over to Cambridge because she wouldn't have been capable of driving herself and there was no one else.

Billy picked up on the third ring - 'I'm coming straight home,' he said and within twenty minutes he was pulling onto the drive.

No one had words of comfort for the other, they held onto one another tightly, as though this would be the last hug they would ever have.

The following day they drove in silence for the horrendous thirty-six miles.

They anxiously waited fifty minutes in the waiting area B before the handsome white haired Mr. Gloom called Ronda through. Billy followed. Mr. Gloom was very Solemn, apologizing for the long wait and the fact they had run out of consulting rooms. He opened a door and led them into a dark room with no windows, it was no larger than a cupboard. It was empty and cold, a treatment bed was positioned along the far wall, but there were no chairs to offer them a seat. Ronda, sat on the edge of the bed, dangling her legs that swung waiting to hear the worst, the air engulfed her lungs like red hot razor blades slicing into her throat as her chest tightened with fear.

Billy stood closely to her side reaching out to hold her hand tightly while Mr. Gloom stood with his arms folded and head bowed low towards Ronda. When they held eye contact, he spoke, but what he said next was unexpected.

'What do you think, you have wrong with you?' he asked. Was he too afraid to say the words, so she had to say them for him?

'It's Cancer, isn't it?' she asked.

'Yes, I am afraid it is and its spread all over your abdomen,' he said as he spread his hand over his own torso.

He proceeded to tell her 'We are not sure if it's safe to operate, so I have re-arranged my surgery appointments for Friday morning so we can take a look inside to see how bad the spread is. The procedure will not include an overnight stay, so I am admitting you as a day patient and you will be well enough to go home later the same day.'

'Will I be put to sleep?' she asked.

'Yes, you will be given a general anesthetic, but rest assured you will not need an overnight bag.

The rest fell on deaf ears, as his voice became a mumbled dribble of words . . . They were only noises, noises that could not be identified as words, words that could not be processed because Ronda wasn't ready to hear them.

It was all too much, too soon, yesterday she was

fine, today she had cancer.

'Can you pull over Billy, I need a pee?'

'Can you hold on until Peterborough services?'

'I will try,' she sniffed through the snot and the tears.

There was a massive queue, women huddled close in a small cubic square of the ladies powder room. Ronda, joined the back of the queue, counting . . . four, five and six she muttered under her breath. Her legs felt weak and wobbly underneath her and the head ache was worsening from that days upset. As deep emotions of past and present colliding invaded her thoughts, Ronda over heated and felt nauseous. The ladies' rest room was warm and stuffy from too many people cramped inside the small space that made it claustrophobic. She had to get out and suddenly she didn't seem quite so desperate to pee anymore.

She removed herself from the queue and pulled the first heavy door to open it. As the door gave way to open, another lady charged in from the second door, leaving the two women trapped in between the two doors for no more than a single minute. As the two women bumped nose to nose, the other woman burst out laughing. However, Ronda had nothing to laugh or even smile about. The women gabbled on with light humour, while Ronda expressed nothing in return.

'You, miserable old cow,' the other women scoffed loudly with a disgruntled tone.

She had no idea what Ronda was going through at that moment in time - if only she had done, maybe she could have been kinder . . .

# Chapter 10

## The following day's
## November 4th and 5th

They went through the following day in a total blur - there seemed so much to do, so many people to tell, The girls, what about the girls?

Of course, no one was going to take the news any other way than badly. Ronda and Billy needed to be strong for their family, but it wasn`t going to be easy.

Ronda and Lizzie dealt with it the only way they knew how and that was with humour. However, Bella and her father did not see any amusement in such devastating news.

It was going to be Billy`s dad`s birthday in a day or two and that was all Ronda could think about. Where on earth was she going to find a couple of warm heavy lumberjack shirts at such short notice now? They decided their best option was the factory shop in Holbeach. So they made it a family day outing with Lizzie and Bella.

Luckily the factory shop had a wide variety of colour choice in his size, so that little problem was soon sorted, it just left a card and a sheet or two of wrapping paper.

The next stop before lunch was Boyes. The shop was busy for a Thursday, there were long queues at the checkout. As they got a little closer to the counter,

Ronda started to smile to herself, 'What's amusing you, Mother?' Bella sniffed.

Her mother took a while to answer, then as Lizzie was the nearest, she asked her to pass a set of false eyelashes to her from the stand at the end of the cosmetic aisle.

Bella looked aghast - 'What on earth do you want those for, Mother?'

'Well,' she said, 'I've been thinking, when I have chemotherapy, it's a fact my hair is going to fall out, the nurse told me yesterday that will include ALL hair,'

'You're not going to start wearing false bloody eyelashes, surely?' her youngest daughter quipped.

As Lizzie passed her a pair, her mother told her, 'No, not those ones - I want those,' pointing to the set that hung on the next hook down.

Lizzie gave her mother an odd look as she unhooked a pair of white plastic fake lashes, with red tips.

Ronda gave her a mischievous grin that told her daughter to play along while they giggled together in the queue.

'Mother, really,' Bella scoffed. 'You can't be flipping serious, for goodness' sake.'

By this time Billy was waiting outside on his phone.

When Lizzie and her mother fell out the door laughing, Bella was not at all amused.

'I don't know how you two can turn this into a comedy act,' she scoffed.

While Billy looked confused, his wife opened the small white paper bag and pulled out the eye lashes. His face had to be so worth the five quid she spent on them.

'Hey Mum, will you lose the hair on your fanny too?' Lizzie chuckled.

Pause . . .

'Hey, once in weaving, twice in weaving, thrice in weaving,' Ronda teased

'What on earth are you on about?' Bella really didn't get the joke, but her sister did and was beside herself trying to control the giggles.

'Well,' her mother explained. I could always save the clumps of hair that fall out and make a postiche!' she laughed.

'Will you two shut up, it's so not funny,' Bella choked, while her father agreed.

'Double sided tape, should do it nicely,' Ronda laughed.

The four of them went to McDonald's for lunch, while Lizzie and her mother continued to make fun, Billy and Bella remained po-faced.

'It's not like you to order so many carbohydrates,' Lizzie told her mother.

'No well, I shall most probably be puking in the bucket once the chemo starts,'

Friday 5th November;

The alarm shocked her as it rang out loudly, it felt as though they had only been sleeping five minutes. Facing such a harrowing day, neither of them had found sleep too easy. It was a windy night that blew from the north, directly into their bedroom window. Ronda felt punch drunk, she wasn't so jolly at this unearthly hour. As the clock ticked to four, she dragged herself to the shower, while Billy went down to make a cup of tea. This was to be the last thing to pass her lips until after it was over.

Surprising enough, she didn't feel one tiny bit perturbed, whereas Billy's belly was churning with anxiety.

Neither of them spoke on the thirty two mile trip to Addenbrookes Hospital, the traffic was minimal at that time of day so they arrived in good time. At least the rain had held off and the wind seemed to have settled, although it came in waves.

They arrived in plenty of time, even the clinic hadn't opened its doors. So, they waited in the entrance hall for another fifteen minutes, by which time several more people had arrived, some with overnight bags, others looking pale and scared. There was a mixture of gender, race and creed, all of whom had concerns of their own.

The time was exactly six thirty in the morning, daylight hadn't broken through. Imagine having to be here this early on five working days? No, Ronda couldn't even try, as far as she was concerned it was still the middle of the night. She had never been an early riser like some folk, maybe if she didn't read until gone midnight, she may find getting out of bed a little easier but a leopard never changes its spots.

Now Ronda was here, the nerves started to surface, so she just sat observing other people, wondering if they felt the same as she did. Billy sat beside her reading yesterday's news paper, he had had very little time or inclination the previous day.

It didn`t seem too long a wait before a doctor called her name. She stood and followed him through to another small windowless box room.

They joined another chap who was the anaesthetist, two very dashing fellas indeed. They were both very kind as they took her medical details, which is the usual protocol before any hospital procedure. For some reason they made her feel a lot calmer.

'The name of the procedure you are having today is called a laparoscopy, a thin lighted tube will be inserted through a small incision in the lower abdomen, here I can look at the ovaries and other pelvic organs and tissue in the area around the bile duct. It will send images of these organs to a video monitor. This will provide a clearer picture that can help plan surgery or other treatments and can help doctors confirm the stage of the cancer, which is how far the tumor has spread. Also, we will be taking biopsies, which are small samples of tissue to be studied further under the microscope. And don`t worry Ronda, we are going to take real good care of you,' they said.

It had been difficult to process the diagnosis, everything was happening at top speed and Ronda, and particularly Billy, hadn`t quite prepared themselves for any of this.

But what was about to happen over the next eight hours was totally unexpected.

Ronda and Billy were led to a cubicle which accommodated two chairs. It offered little privacy, only a curtain divided the small space from that of the patients who sat either side of them. She changed into a theatre gown, that was open at the back apart from the ties that ran each side of the opening. Billy tied these in double bows to eliminate the risk of them coming undone. She was given paper pants to wear underneath and a paper hat to cover her hair. All make-up, nail varnish, and jewellery were to be removed and her wedding ring was taped over by the nurse.

Ronda was nil by mouth, so she wasn`t able to join Billy in a chocolate bar or cup of tea to kill some of the waiting time.

At least it wasn`t long before Ronda was taken through to the operating theatre. She walked along the corridor clutching the back of her gown to avoid it flapping open to reveal her big girl paper pants underneath, following the nurse who led her to the double doors at the far end that read 'Do not enter, operation in process.' It was a small room where she met the anesthetist again, this time he was wearing his scrubs including a face mask, but he had the most amazing dark brown eyes she had ever seen. And when he smiled underneath the mask, his eyes sparkled, instantly she knew it was him before he even spoke. He took hold of her hand and stroked it gently while he spoke to her calmly.

'How are you feeling?' he asked kindly.

'Okay, I think,' she replied.

As he repeated the same words he had spoken to her earlier, he said, 'I don`t want you to worry about a thing, we are going to take real good care of you,'

How could she not trust those eyes - she trusted him

beyond all measures.

'Well,' she said, 'if I die now, I will die happy,' and then she laughed.

His eyes creased as he laughed too, 'You are not going to die,' he promised.

And then she fell silent . . .

Billy, was pacing the floor like a lost lamb waiting to be slaughtered, there is only so much coffee one can consume in these situations, so he decided to take a walk around the hospital grounds. There were miles of corridor alone without the perimeter of the outside building.

Today most people would be planning their bonfire party or attending fire work displays, children would be excited and dressing up for their guying expedition.

*'Please can you remember the fifth of November, the poor old me, with the grim in my tummy, a hole in my belly, please can you spare me a prayer or two. If you haven't got a prayer, just a thought will do and if you haven't got a thought, then God Bless You.'*

Each time Billy glanced at his watch only a few minutes had passed. He was feeling restless as he dreaded the outcome.

He fumbled inside his back pocket for his phone, but it wasn't there. He checked the inside of his coat pocket, it wasn't there either. Where was his damn phone?

He decided he should wander back to the car, to check inside. The car was parked on the multi-story car park on the edge of the hospital. His car was on the third floor up, so he took the lift. As the doors opened, a chap with his loved one in a wheel chair barged in front. 'Oh, don't mind me,' Billy scoffed. He decided to wait for the next lift, he hardly wanted to be in a confined space with someone as rude as that - when he was feeling a delicate wreck. He would either express weakness or thump the old geezer where it hurt.

By the time he finally reached his car, he could hear the faint ring of a mobile phone. It was Billy's phone; he clicked his fob to open the door and reached for his phone from the passenger seat.

It was a strange number, not one to be recognized. He was actually expecting one of the girls to be calling to ask how things were going with their mother. He picked up, 'Billy Stone speaking how may I help you?'

'Hello Billy, John Gloom speaking, I am calling you from the operating theatre. Your wife is in good hands and the laparoscopy has told us what we need to know, the results of our findings are as expected, but while we thought she would need three rounds of chemo to shrink the tumour before major surgery could commence, we now feel that it would be in Ronda's best interest to go ahead with the operation NOW.'

'Okay,' Billy said in a stunned shaky voice.

'Thing is Billy, we need your consent to go ahead.'

'Err, yes, yes of course, do whatever is best.'

'We need to do a full hysterectomy which consists of the removal of her ovaries, fallopian tubes, womb, and cervix.'

'Yes of course,' Billy answered quietly.

'There has also been some spread to the edge of her bowl, so we need to remove a small part - this will not affect her in any way what so ever. We will remove her appendix, although there doesn't seem to be any disease found in the appendix, it isn`t something your wife needs and it is just somewhere else for the disease to spread in time if we leave it, it's best out than in, to be honest.'

'Okay.'

'And we will remove her omentum, which is a thin fold of abdominal tissue that encases the stomach, the large intestine and the other abdominal organs. This fatty lining contains lymph nodes, lymph vessels, nerves and blood vessels. It is perfectly normal to find cancerous cells in the omentrum with a stage 3-4 cancer, so can we please operate NOW?

'Well, yes, yes please do.'

'It`s border line operable, but it will offer your wife the best possible prognosis,

cancers at such an advanced stage can escalate very quickly overnight.'

Pause … 'Are we agreed?' he asked again.

'Yes of course.' Billy agreed with finality.

Mr. Gloom thanked him and the line went dead.'

Billy stood on the spot, unable to move, he came over dizzy as everything fell in a haze around him. Had he just dreamt it all or was this really happening right now?

Why was it an emergency? Didn`t these things only happen on TV? He recalled the surgeons phoning a loved one with news, from the operating theatre on some hospital series and now it was happening in real life. How could this be? It was too much, too much too soon. His head ached and his brain turned to mash as he tried to process the implications of that telephone call.

As Billy collapsed on the passenger seat, he cried in his cupped hands, now he understood why operations were cancelled in the final hour. It's about someone else more needy - he felt very honoured to think they wanted to do whatever it took to save Ronda from the dreaded C.

Fear started to close in on him as he was overwhelmed by the thought of women who actually die having this surgery. He panicked - he hadn't told her how much he loved her, how beautiful she was, how he couldn't live without her.

'Pull yourself together,' he triple stammered inside his own head.

*How dare that ignorant, arrogant gynaecologist from the previous week be such a PIG?*

He was unsure what to do now, this would be a two-to-five-hour operation, not to mention how long she would be in recovery. What about her night clothes, toothbrush, she would be needing all of those things? Was he right to assume his wife's surgeon would phone again once she was out of surgery?

Should he drive home or should he wait? He decided to wait until he knew she was out of danger and then he would drive back to Spalding to collect some things for her stay in hospital. In the meantime, he would go to the main concourse to have a Costa Coffee and lunch from Burger King.

Having some food inside his belly made him feel a lot better, he was calmer now, and more at ease as he started to realise this way was for the best because it prevented all the anxiety and sleepless nights while they waited for a surgery date.

Time soon passed, he read the paper from cover to cover, he sat with a third coffee as he people watched. He even thought about getting his hair cut or booking a holiday. They had everything in the concourse. It was like a shopping centre in itself, and it was busy too.

He checked for messages but there weren't any. He wanted to phone the girls to bring them up to speed but decided to wait until Ronda was safe.

He felt his body tightening from all the stress so decided to go for another wander around the hospital to kill time more than anything.

As he wandered along the busy corridor dodging the students who rushed with speed to get from a to b, some on their phones others chatting to their peers, hospital porters transferring patients in wheel chairs or hospital beds; doctors and nurses colliding with one another, made Billy feel quite disorientated.

Then suddenly with no warning, a grey-haired chap greeted him with a smile. It was Mr. Gloom, still wearing his scrubs; He offered Billy a hand shake, your wife has done well, her surgery went to plan, I have her in the best possible hands and care of the Mcmillan surgeon, who was my right-hand man. She will be in recovery for a little while but someone can let you know when she is on the ward. Then you can see her.

'Thank you, thank you so much,' Billy cried and laughed in the same breath.

'She didn't bring an overnight case,' Billy told him.

'She will be fine until you visit tomorrow,' he assured him. 'Phone your family and tell them the good news.'

'Good news?' Billy quizzed.

'Yes, it's excellent news, the cancer has all gone.'

'And chemo?' Billy asked, getting ahead of himself.

'She will need six rounds of intravenous chemotherapy to make sure the bugger doesn't come back for a very long time.' he said with certainty.

Billy felt as though all his Christmases and birthdays had come at once.

But phew, what a day!

*'Time to tell the kids.'*

# Chapter 11

## 'Recovery.'

She heard a distant clatter of obstacles, coming from far, far away. She could detect muffled voices but it was all too vague and undefined.

She was unable to move or speak but she didn't care to try. She drifted in and out of consciousness until the anesthetic weakened. This wasn't a feeling that she recognized through the strangeness of this elusive reality. The fog deep inside her own head circled brief moments of clarity in a dim misty halo before her very eyes.

Her eyes flickered open again. She felt dazzled by the brightness of the light, she could not distinguish where she was or why as she tried to make sense of the peculiar noises around her, heavy whispers, punctured by bleeps, grazed by a constant, low-pitched hum. Then she realized she was in hospital. She was lying down, that much was clear, and without trying she knew she couldn't get up.

She heard a voice then realized it was her own, as she cried out in pain.

'Ronda, can you hear me pet?'

As she blinked slowly, 'Ronda are you back with us?'

Ronda was too apathetic to stir, she became aware of the nurse taking her OBS, but she had no desire to open her eyes, or speak, all she wanted to do was sleep.

She wanted to be left alone and sleep forever.

She had no idea how long it was before she woke with such a gripping pain in her belly, it was like severe period pains or cramps, only one hundred times worse.

It was as severe as labour but this didn't waver, it was strong and intense and it did not peak or trough, it just remained stronger than she could bare without crying out.

She felt a sudden, desperate need for her mother, so powerful that she wanted to call out her name, but her voice was a small stifled moan inside the mask over her mouth.

The pain was gripping, 'Dear Jesus,' she thought, 'if it's this bad having a laparoscopy, how bad could it be when they cut her open to remove the whole contents of her pelvise?' There was no one to ask and of course she had no idea, how they had mutilated her body to save her. Little did she know, she was no longer a woman, she wasn't anything now, just an IT! At least that's how she would feel.

As she tried to save her dignity and sobbed into her pillow with teeth clenched into it, she bit hard, as though her life depended upon it. The groans hadn't gone unnoticed and the theatre nurse rushed to her side.

'Ah you're awake pet, so you are, what's the matter, pet? Are you in pain? Where does it hurt, pet?'

'In my womb,' Ronda cried through gritted teeth.

'Ah no, pet, it's not in your womb, you no longer have a womb, pet.'

'What?' Ronda mumbled, 'I don`t understand.'

The nurse had a kind face, her voice was reassuring.

'It`s gone, pet, they took it all out, pet, you`ve not got a womb no more, they did the big operation, it's all over and your cancer has gone.'

The lovely nurse from Northumberland, gave her the morphine pump and told her to press it as often as she needed it. The relief was immense as she soon felt the pain slide away. She became very tired again and must have gone back to sleep.

She had no idea how long it had been before she felt this intense feeling of falling. She gasped as her blurry eyes opened. It took a while to gain focus, the lights above were bright and dazzling.

She could feel a weird kind of motion as though she was moving from side to side then suddenly swung in the opposite direction, then back again. Her head was spinning with dizziness and fatigue. Then she became aware of noise, it was the sound of voices chattering but the voices were not defined or clear enough to understand what anyone was saying. She managed to raise her head from the soft pillow beneath her, it pulled tight around her belly. Remembering the words as she felt tears sting her eyes, she realized where she was and why. What was going to happen to her now? Who was she? Where was her mother.'

It was the same nurse who she remembered speaking to before.

'By heck, you've had a nice long sleep. We are just moving you up to the ward Ronda pet.'

'What about Billy?' she said in a panic as she remembered.

'Who`s Billy?' the nurse asked.

'My husband, he'll be worried.'

'Mr. Gloom has already spoken to your husband, he will be waiting for you up on the ward, pet.'

Suddenly the adrenalin took over and Ronda went as high as a kite. She started to tell the nurses some hilarious jokes, which had them in stitches laughing.

But Ronda didn't know any jokes, she was known for not being very good at understanding them, let alone remembering any of them. She could be at a party with jokes flying around her ears and Ronda would be the only person who wasn't in hysterics. It was as though she had suddenly had a personality transplant.

'She's a bit high,' the nurse warned Billy. 'Don't worry pet, it'll be the anesthetic, that's all it'll be.'

'Calm down,' Billy scoffed out of embarrassment.

'Don't tell her that,' the nurse laughed, 'She's had us entertained, we've all been in stitches.'

But Billy didn't seem impressed, how could she be so high, when he felt as though his whole world was falling apart. For Christ's sake, what was there to laugh about at a time like this?

'Don't knock it, expect her to come down with a bang later, it's all perfectly normal,' the nurse explained. 'But she won't remember any of this later,' she told him.

Ronda closed her eyes and felt the relief of giving into exhaustion - It was so much easier than trying to fight it.

The nurse was right, her journey back from the

theatre to the ward soon became a misty haze.

Her five days stay in hospital was simply awful, other patients came and went, some snored loudly, while others watched TV all hours throughout the day and night. One lady cried a lot, another coughed all the time. One kept throwing up, another constantly pooed herself. The women in the bed opposite Ronda stared at her, as soon as Ronda glanced back, the women started to speak, 'What's your name? My name is Janet, I've been brave I have.' Ronda was too lethargic to speak, she just wanted this 'brave person' to shut the fuck up and stop starring.

The lady sat at Janet's bedside offered her apologies. Ronda couldn't bare to look at her, let alone try to hold a decent conversation with her.

When the doctors did their rounds, curtains were drawn around beds for privacy but there was no privacy, the doctors talked loudly and everyone could hear every single word spoken. One lady had breast cancer, another cancer of the vagina and one had cancer of the ear. The two elderly ladies had kidney failure and were taken away several times for dialysis. It was grim and Ronda could only think about death! The nurse had been right, Ronda did come down with a bang, she cried a lot and was in a lot of pain and discomfort. She made a promise she would NEVER complain about her fibromyalgia pain again.

The sixty-mile journey home from Addenbrookes hospital was horrendous, Billy drove really steadily but Ronda was feeling every single bump in the road.

It was wonderful to be pulling on their drive two hours later, but it was agony to get out of the car to the front door. Shattered by trauma and exhaustion, her final mission was getting up the stairs to her own bed.

She took herself straight to the spare bedroom, knowing she would rest better sleeping alone. *Bugger, it was good to be home!*

It also felt extremely scary, there was no home care other than what Billy could do. None of this was for the faint at heart, she was in so much pain and each day she faced another new challenge.

There was no follow up appointment, no doctors visit, no district nurse - or at least not at first. Then things changed as Ronda developed an infection.

Six weeks passed before her appointment with the oncologist to discuss her chemotherapy regime, and this was when she started to live with the after math of cancer.

Suddenly Ronda and Billy realized this was not something you can just sweep under the carpet and get on with your life just because the cancer had been cut out of you.

It would be a forever, ongoing fear. The highs and lows with each impact would leave them feeling floored over and over and over again.

No one knew what her future would hold, how far she would have to run to reach the end of line. How many hurdles she would have to jump, with a few bruised knees each time she didn't jump quite high enough.

There were psychological issues to come to terms with, no one offered counselling, few seemed to care. They felt as though they were left to fend for themselves and the overwhelming isolation of it all was far too surreal to even go there.

She didn't want to connect with anyone's pity. She understood they were sorry, that everyone was anxious to come and see her, but there was nothing they could do or say to make any of this shit go away. But she didn't want them to try. It would only make matters worse. Worse would be if they didn't care enough to be anxious too.

Everyone had her best interest at heart, but it didn't take away the loneliness, of the hours in the dark when she was too exhausted to sleep. When the pain was so bad she simply wanted it all to end.

The only person that talked any sense was Judith, her dental nurse who told her, 'You can`t be brave all the time, allow yourself to grieve for the part of you that is now missing.' She totally seemed to get it!

# Chapter 12

## 'Chemotherapy'

Ronda was diagnosed with Serous Ovarian Cancer which was staged at a 3.

Cancer is staged - 1A, 1B, 1C, 2A, 2B, 2C, 3 A, 3B, 3C and 4.

Ronda started her chemotherapy with Paclitaxel and Carboplatin, both particularly toxic drugs. Taxol is derived from the yew trees and carbo from platinum, both killers in their own right! Luckily for Ronda the steroids supported the anti-sickness regime.

The constant bleeping reminded Ronda why she was here. It was incredible really, that the drip in her vein played a vital part in keeping her alive.

The other part, she knew, had to come from her.

She needed to find the energy and determination to get through this, even beat it if she could.

She was aware what everyone else was thinking - the cancer has gone, so what's the big deal? Why sweat the small stuff? Although Ronda knew in reality how impossible that was going to be.

Even so, didn't she owe it to herself to make the time she had left as special and uplifting as she could for those she loved?

Everyone assumes the chemotherapy clinic would be a depressing place, with every single person of all ages, genders, and creed fighting their life-threatening disease.

Reaching out to search the picture in her mind, as

her third eye takes focus of her own imagination. Her vision is of weak thin, pale faced patients, with bald heads and turbans as they drag their legs with a shuffle gripping tightly to their drip towards the bathroom, to take another pee. Well, it's kind of like that, but it is fair to say that most people make an extra special effort to 'Dress-Up,' for the occasion - patients claim it makes them feel better. And most importantly it helps them party!

Yes indeed, that is correct 'PARTY!'

Everyone's cancer is different, everyone is fighting a different stage. Some would be starting out on their journey, while others were close to the end of life.

*'But, on the chemo ward depressing and sad it never was.'*

A great many of them were prescribed steroids, but that was as far as the happy drugs went, as far as I am aware it wasn't common practice to prescribe mood enhancers to cancer patients. And they were hardly ever offered a brandy in their cup of tea at refreshment time. However, like a party, it kind of was. The chemo ward was far from depressing.

It was a friendly atmosphere; they were like one big happy family. Everyone referred to one another by first names and the love radiated between the nursing staff and their patients.

'Short Sharp Scratch.'

'You always say that,' Lynn said while she sat on one of the pink chairs, 'and I never feel a thing.'

'That's because she's a good nurse,' Peter chipped in from the yellow chair.

'I ruddy well should be I've been doing this job for over thirty years.' Judith chuckled.

'Turn the radio up Anne, I like this tune,' Christine announced from the red team.

Instantly, Christine burst into song, but sing she could not, did she care, not!

The patients soon started to join in and Christine started to do a merry jig around the floor.

A couple of other nurses joined in, including the ward matron, while the rest giggled to encourage them.

'You lot `aving a party in `ere? I can `ere you down the corridor,' the next patient asked, as she booked herself in at the reception desk for her treatment.

'Everyday's a party, when you ain`t got long to live,' Charles announced.

'Hay we won`t `ave that talk in `ere, none of us are going to snuff it today.'

'Too right,' Margaret said. 'We ain`t going nowhere.'

'We need to keep smiling, cos unless we have an `appy face, they won`t let us in at the pearly gates.'

'Full name, date of birth,' Nurse Adam asked his patient sitting in one of the blue chairs.

'Rebecca Smith, 14-10-1968.'

'Super,' Adam said as he tied the patient's wrist band around her thin skeletal wrist.

A sudden co-motion was heard from one of Judith's

yellow chairs.

'Oh my God - shit, shit, shit' Ronda screamed as she jumped out of her yellow chair holding onto her backside as though her life depended on it.

Immediately Judith started to apologize. 'I am so, so sorry,' Judith was close to tears when she realized exactly what she had done wrong, leaving poor Ronda dancing around with her hands down the back of her pants, clutching onto her bare flesh.

By complete accident Judith had squirted one of the pretreatment drugs into Ronda's cannula in one quick shot, when it should be administered nice and slowly to prevent this very painful stinging nettle side effect.

'I am so sorry,' Judith apologized again and again. 'I have been doing this job for over 30 years and I have never, ever made that mistake before in my life.'

'About time you retired then, in it?' Peter chuckled from one of the other yellow chairs. 'Ow old a yer?'

'It's because everyone has been distracting her with too much larking about,' Gertrude announced from her pink chair. 'She's a good nurse remember.'

'It's okay nobody died,' Ronda chuckled as the pain was quickly starting to wane.

Billy sat belly laughing his head off until tears fell. Even Ronda couldn't straighten up for laughing so hard.

Later that night in bed, Billy started to laugh out loud as he thought about the fun six hours entertainment he had enjoyed while his wife was dancing around in agony. He could barely get the words out.

'I have never witnessed anything as funny in all my days, all I could think of was that cat from the Tom and Jerry cartoon when he had sat on red hot coals. You even wailed like him.'

'It flipping well hurt, oh my God the pain.'

*'Then there was the WIG, Oh My God the WIG!'*

# Chapter 13

## 'The WIG'

Summoning the strength again, Ronda swung her feet slowly to the floor and inhaled a deep, steadying breath. It took a moment for the dizziness to pass, leaving a surprising but welcome feeling of calm.

The thought of her hair falling out on the pillow and blocking up the shower revolted her. The only way was to shave it all off. But she couldn't expect Lizzie or Bella to do it, it'd be too upsetting for them.

Then someone suggested a local hairdresser who was going into wigs, well Ronda needed a wig, so she selected a few from his brochure, he ordered them and Ronda chose the one she liked the best. Frank also offered to do the head shave and fit the new wig. So, while she was in recovery from the massive operation this gave her something to focus on. Bella insisted on taking her because she wasn't able to drive for eight weeks; not that Bella was happy about her mother's driving at the best of times.

Ronda, didn't want fame or fortune but she saw this as something positive. And the rest just seemed to happen on its own accord, she raised a whopping one thousand pounds for Cancer Research U.K. and a bit for Mcmillan. There was a little left over to buy some small electric blankets, that are used in the chemo ward to warm up patients collapsed veins which helped the nurses get a line in. It was well worth it, even Bella's tears. People who she had never met before even donated, everyone was so generous.

Things like this, help people to get through the many challenges ahead.

It gives every step a purpose and if the grim can be turned into something good then so be it. It releases adrenaline that helps to heal and cope better - even better than steroids.

The wig was fabulous, even shop assistants asked where she got her hair highlighted and cut. They could not believe it when she told them it was a wig.

Now, you may wonder what is the point in wearing false hair if you're going to tell all and sundry it's a wig?

Well, if you think like that, you have a good point, Ronda didn't actually announce it to the world however, she thought it helped a lot of ladies. One friend said she'd sooner lose a breast than her hair. Well, hair grows back, breasts do not, but for her it would be the bigger issue. Once she saw the transformation from bald to wig, she was so impressed it took that particular fear of cancer away.

Some people, prefer to go natural regardless of the hair loss and that's ok, people tend to be much nicer, they open doors, offer their seat. And if that's the way to go, they do some fabulous head scarves, in the most amazing designs and colours.

The positive of having no hair is the fact that you don't

ever have a bad hair day, you get up wash head in the shower, rub with a towel, job sorted, so much easier when you are feeling groggy from the side effects of chemo.

Another thing is people don't often realize you also lose the whole of your body hair. Now, that is also a big bonus, no more shaving, plucking, epilating, waxing or anything else you desire to do to get rid of unwanted hair. This is wonderful in the summer months, think about the time and money paid out on hair removers and hairdresser's bills. Your skin becomes so transparent it feels like a baby's bum, all over. So, there are many ways how you can turn the negative into a positive.

Ronda also noticed how her skin tanned without even looking at the sun, it just seemed to change the pigment in her skin and she embraced the freckles as though it was just another beautiful creation of God's magic.

When Ronda`s hair started to grow back, it was as a grey as a cloudy day and she hated it. The down side to wigs is they do make you very hot, it's like wearing a woolly hat indoors, and the effects of an instant menopause did not help the ongoing head sweats. That was the down side, but not everyone burns up like Ronda did, so if it's winter and you feel the cold you`ll be fine. Wigs also make your head itch so to wear them all the time is going to be a bit tough sometimes, but hey-ho, on the whole Ronda just loved them, they were fun and she enjoyed wearing a new look every day. Over a period of time, she collected a total of eight fabulous wigs. One day the short blond bob would be her favourite, another day it would be the bubble gum wig, that had a shimmer of very pale pink, which was such fun to wear and it made her feel younger. Her very short graduated bob in pearl blonde and dark brown roots gave a glow of pale blue and baby green highlights, not many but enough to help her feel fabulous on one of her darkest of days.

The wigs were great - they could be washed by hand in the bowl and blot dried in a rolled-up towel. They were simply left to dry overnight on a wig stand, with no styling or brushing. By morning they were ready to wear after a quick shake and the locks fell back into shape. This is one of the best things about synthetic wigs.

Real wigs may be more expensive, they may be easier to cut or style but they also need to be blow dried into shape like anyone's real hair does. Go out in the wind or on a misty day the style will drop, frizz, curl or hang long and lank. They lose their va-va-voom, in all weather conditions. They even split and dry out in the sun. One bonus to real hair is you can colour them, perm them and have a restyle but remember they won`t grow again when you decide it's too short. And if you change the colour too many times they will also suffer the effects of chemical damage and they will always need quite a few hair products to keep them healthy.

You are not going to need a wig for long, your natural hair grows back very quickly once you have finished the chemo. But unless the pixi look really suits you, it`ll be a good year before you get a very short bob back.

You can buy a really nice synthetic wig for less than a hundred pound. Cost greatly depends on the weight and length. Always choose a light weight wig for the warmer months of the year, wigs that are very heavy can cause a headache and it's important to find a good fit.

Your oncologist will usually give you an NHS prescription for a wig, most hospitals have a wig supplier who has a salon in the hospital where you can select the right wig for you. Help and advice is always at hand but the prescription doesn`t always cover the full cost and you may need to ask your oncologist if you qualify for a wig. You only get one on the NHS, although because Ronda`s first chemo treatment was eight years before her re-occurrence, she was eligible for a second NHS wig.

Ronda bought a really nice stylish layered wig for her godson's wedding. It was a poor fit and it kept riding up, so she developed this nasty habit of grabbing hold of the sides and pulling it down. It certainly caused a bit of attention in the restaurant her friend took her to, I suppose it would have looked a bit odd, and rather confusing to see a lady of mature years moving her hair around her scalp.

Also this wig, had large mesh holes, the whole purpose was to make it cooler to wear in the heat wave of the Spring 2011. But as it kept rising up, it was rather baggy on the top of her head, so she also wore a feathered fascinator to help secure it in place, which it did - but . . .

Ronda`s godson and his beautiful bride married at a

pretty little church in the village where his bride lived with her parents. It was such a hot day, and wearing hats and tights made everyone feel uncomfortable, but imagine wearing a woolly hat underneath one's fascinator!

First Billy and Ronda were late because Ronda had to keep taking cool showers to cool off, otherwise she'd be stinky before they got to the flipping church. She would have been much more comfortable in one of her cool summer dresses, without all the fancy stuff. I think that was the first time ever she didn't want to get dressed up.

Anyway, they made it by the skin of their teeth, and the wedding was beautiful.

Like all weddings every one chatted while the photos are being taken, the wedding venue was held at a beautiful hall in Cambridgeshire, and the gardens were lovely for the photo shoot. They stood around chatting to friends as they drank a cold glass of bubbly, the men a beer, and were eventually called into the great hall to be seated for the reception.

They slowly followed a good number of people from the garden to the decking area.

Thankfully, God does give mercy sometimes because luckily, they were the last four guests to go inside, as they walked under the beautiful arch of climbing roses, Ronda felt a tug on her head and suddenly there was a cool refreshing draft. Her natural instinct was to stroke her hair, but holy ruddy Moses, all she could feel, was skin!

The bramble had caught under the mesh of the wig, and as she walked on, it pulled the wig clean off her scalp - fascinator included. The twig and attached hair piece flew into the air, leaving it neatly swinging eight foot high in the top of the rose tree.

It could only happen to Ronda!

It was one of those situations when you either have hysterics and leave the party in floods of tears or you laugh!

Well, Ronda was quite tipsy on the orange juice, so she really did not care. She could do nothing but giggle, the look on people's faces was a picture of shock and horror especially from the ladies. The young girl carrying a tray of empty glasses almost dropped them, Billy started apologizing to everyone, explaining how his wife had just finished chemotherapy.

While, Ronda just stood waiting for someone, anyone, to reach for her wig so she could quickly cover up before too many other people wondered what all the commotion was about. It all happened so fast, talk about letting her hair down, Ronda's giggles soon became a hysterical moment of fun time. She laughed so hard she didn't quite know how to stop. Finally, Billy reached for the wig, her best friend Sharon handed her a small compact mirror from her bag, drying her eyes she sniffled her tears, and said 'You looked so beautiful darling and no one could have ever known that was a wig.'

'Well, they fecking well do now, don't they?'

Ronda chortled in humour. 'Oh Billy, get me a drink,' she asked before breaking out into another fit of giggles.

So, cancer doesn't always need to be grim, or at least not all the time - Ronda decided to make the most of it. Hopefully, this will be one of the funniest stories that will continue to be told long after she has gone.

. . .

When someone you know starts to grow their hair back, it'll look grey and manly, you don`t ask them, 'What on earth have you done to your hair?' like someone asked Ronda one day in Morisons's supermarket.

She may not have wanted to say she was growing her hair back after chemotherapy took it away. Sometimes, she felt as though she had just been through enough and now at last, she felt she had started to turn a corner and bring some normality back into her life. She shouldn't have felt the need to justify how the grey pixi look made her suddenly gain twenty years in age. But more to the point, how rude was he?

Another person seemed to break their neck to tell her once she had grown her blonde bob back, how much better it looked than the dull mousy grey curls.

The truth was Ronda already knew that without someone actually bringing it to her attention.

She reacted bluntly, by putting them in their place, 'Well, I hardly had a choice, did I, she chided.

'Oh, I know that,' was their reply.

Ronda wondered what their point was - if she knew she had no flipping choice, I mean why pass a silly and hurtful comment like that?

Some people simply have no tact.

That said on the whole people were truly wonderful and that made so much of a difference and Ronda was determined not to let the silly comments from small minded people out-weigh the positive ones.

Ronda continued to have three monthly oncology checkups, which basically was a blood test and a chat, then after three years, the appointments became six monthly. After five years she was discharged from oncology and that's when it all started to feel scary.

Suddenly Ronda felt alone with fears and thoughts that had been buried deeply in her heart.

As far as everyone else was concerned her battle was over, they had cured her completely and she was a very lucky person. But why did she feel this would never be over.

Ronda's brother Neil had lost his fight against colon cancer and that broke her heart. Ronda and her brother were so incredibly different they never stayed in touch very often during their adult life. But they never once argued and he never once failed to call her on Christmas morning. He always ended the call by telling her he loved her. Ronda had a lot of issues when Neil lost his battle with the death eater. She went through survival guilt, and a whole lot more.

The day of Neil's funeral took place on Tuesday 3<sup>rd</sup> April, 2012 at twelve - fifteen in the afternoon.

It was a sight to be remembered. Ronda had never been to a civil service before. This felt oddly strange since they had both been brought up with church on a Sunday.

As Ronda stood with her family outside the small chapel at the crematorium the sound of motor bike engines hummed from a distance. The sound became louder as the hum followed Ronda's brother slowly. He had chosen a cardboard coffin with a tranquil scene of blue skies along a river bank, with fishermen sitting patiently waiting for a catch. It was beautiful and represented Neil very well.

The mourners followed Neil into the chapel, or as many who could get in the doors. The pews were soon taken up, other mourners stood in the aisle to pay their respects.

Ronda had never seen such a display of skin-headed, tattooed heads, faces, necks, bodies and limbs in all her days, and the body piercings were on another level. Some had long hair and plaited beards and all those members of the motor bike club with whom her brother was a huge part of must have been roasting in their leathers. It was weirdly amazing.

People oozed out of the door. Mourners cried, they laughed too at shared memories because those who knew Ronda's brother would have known some of his ways, he certainly was unique and there was never a dull moment while he was around. He could light up a darken room without a candle.

He came in to 'Set Fire to the Rain' by Adele.

Music for reflection he chose, 'Comfortably Numb' by Pink Floyd.

The closing music, Neil's choice was 'Fire Fighter' by Prodigy.

It made everyone smile because that was Neil!

Ronda suddenly felt alone, with no mum, no dad and now her brother gone. When you are a child, you can never imagine being the one to be left behind, but if you have been blessed and lucky in love then you may be lucky enough to make a new family through marriage and children and lots of friends, you need not to worry because you will never walk alone as once you would have imagined.

Nothing is ever as bad as you imagine. Challenges life send our way are only given to strengthen us; you'll be surprised where that strength can come from.

*It was beautiful as long as it lasted*
*The journey of my life.*
*I have no regrets whatsoever save*
*The pain I leave behind.*
*Those dear hearts who love and care . . .*
*The strong arms who held me up*
*when my own strength let me down.*
*At every turning of my life*
*I came across good friends,*
*Friends who stood by me*
*Even when the time raced me by.*

*Farewell, farewell my friends*
*I smile and bid you goodbye.*
*No, shed no tears for I need them not*
*All I need is your smile.*
*If you feel sad do think of me*
*For that is what I`ll like.*
*When you live in the hearts of those you love*
*Remember then you never die.*

'Farewell My Friends' – Rabindranath Tagore

The following eight years passed too quickly but it was filled to the brim with adventures and joy. Ronda tried to embrace every day with a breath of gratitude. She started to appreciate things a lot more than she once would have taken for granted.

Ronda and Billy didn't have the holidays they once had because that wasn't on their agenda now. Her chronic illness sucked away a great portion of her energy, as it often plagued her with pain and profound fatigue. It was now just too big a thing to jump the milestone of travel. Whereas once she loved the holidays, now she just dreaded the thought of them. But Billy and Ronda enjoyed some fabulous days out and they made the most of everyday as though it was their last.

Billy took early retirement before Ronda had finished her treatment and they never got tired of being around one another. Billy had his darts twice a week, accompanied by friendship and beer. He played golf every Sunday, unless it rained.

Ronda continued with her painting, knitting and sewing. Life was most enjoyable.

She continued to look after Lizzie's little boy, Thomas, until he started school. Bella announced she was expecting her first baby girl after a short while on fertility treatment. Ellenor, was named after Ellenor Worfe, Ronda's maternal grandmother, which was rather special.

A couple of years later, Lizzie married and moved on to have another child, a beautiful little girl, they called her Molly Grace.

Then in 2016 Billy and Ronda supported Bella through her IVF treatment and a year later Bella gave birth to a beautiful baby boy' Jake, and now their families were complete.

The three families moved homes, Ronda and Billy moved into a new build the other side of town, to gain a bit more space. Bella moved into Ronda and Billy's family home with her own family, and Lizzie and family moved into a much bigger home too. This made so much difference to everyone's life and it couldn't get any better than that. Sometimes Ronda would wake up, knowing how lucky she was to achieve all the wonderful things her own mum and grandmother were denied.

As time passed Ronda and Billy had moved on from the cancer, Ronda worried less about it returning, *maybe she really had been cured?*

Everything about the past few years of her life had been positive and then it all started to change again and it hit the family like a boulder out of the sky.

*'In 2019 after eight years in remission, **the grim returned with avengeance.**'*

# Chapter 14

## 'BRCA'

'WHAT, the dickens is BRCA one?' I hear you say!

Well, let me explain, in layman's terms, otherwise you'll most probably get lost with all the gobble-dee-gook of fancy words you may not have heard before.

The BRCA gene is your defence against cancer. Everyone has the BRCA gene, it's part of our DNA. When you are born your cells are replaced at a rapid speed, this is needed to help with our growing process. Then once we are fully grown, the speed of our cell growth slows down. And our new cells replace old cells as they die.

A great majority of people who have a healthy DNA, have no problem with their gene functioning as it should do. This means that your healthy BRCA gene makes sure your cells do not mutate, as the older cells you no longer need are destroyed, and replaced with new ones.

However, for those such as Ronda and her two daughters who have inherited the faulty BRCA gene, it means that they have slight damage to their DNA. This means that their BRCA gene doesn't function as it should therefore their defence against fighting cancer cells is compromised.

As we age this process speeds up again, but the new

cells grow far faster than the old ones die and we therefore end up with too many. The cells that our body has no use for begin to clump together as they mutate, leaving a 50% risk of developing ovarian cancerous tumors; also, a whopping 85% risk of developing breast cancer.

The only way to prevent developing these cancers is by radical invasive surgeries, by removing those organs that are most likely to be affected.

But how do we know if we have this damaged DNA? Well, if you have several ladies running down your maternal blood line with a breast or ovarian cancer history, then you qualify to have the test. This is when it becomes really complicated.

Ronda had always feared getting ovarian cancer, she lost her own mother to this horrific disease when she was just fourty-seven. Ronda had no family history other than her own mother as far as she could possibly know, and no history of breast cancer as far as she was aware.

She had always been concerned about her own health; this fear increased tenfold once she reached the age of forty. Ronda's GP was fully aware of her fears and told her she was quite right to be concerned, however at the time there was no available screening for ovarian cancer, and Ronda was classed as too young to have routine yearly breast screening.

At this time the test had not been licensed and Cancer Research were only just looking into genetics and why these particular cancers tend to run in some families and not others.

Thankfully, Ronda's oncologist immediately requested the test as soon as it was available. This needed to be done very quickly and she had no time for the usual routine of medical counselling from the genetic team, that would need to come later. Her test needed to be done before she started the chemotherapy treatment. This is because chemotherapy destroys that part of our DNA. The part of our DNA that repairs damaged cells.

As soon as her test came back positive for BRCA One Ronda was referred for genetic counselling, and her brother was contacted by the genetic team to ask if he was prepared to also have the test. At that time Ronda's brother was fighting colon cancer. His test proved negative, this told medical science that Neil's cancer was not caused by the faulty BRCA one. Therefore, Neil's three children would not qualify for the test. However, Ronda's girls did, now they were faced with the personal decision of deciding whether or not to go for it.

Of course, if one decided to have the test and the other didn't, or one carried the faulty DNA and the other didn't, it could cause a lot of anxiety for the family.

Thankfully, both daughters needed to know if they had it or not.

This added to a great deal of worry and stress. What if one carried it and the other didn't? Sadly, they both tested BRCA One positive.

There is also a BRCA 2 gene mutation and maybe even a 3 by now.

The genetic team talked Ronda through her options and she decided it was a no brainier. It was too late to prevent ovarian cancer by having healthy organs removed, but it wasn't too late to prevent breast cancer. Having a double mastectomy lowered her risk from 85% down to 3%. She had no other choice but to have the brutal operation of a double mastectomy. This felt like a mutilation of her own body and it wasn`t a choice she would wish anyone to go through. However, Ronda could see no other way. She had a great deal to think about. Was she scared? Yes, of course she was scared: she was petrified.

The only other option was yearly screening but that wouldn't prevent breast cancer, it may help to catch it early, but that's about it.

What choice did she have? The odds either way felt against her.

Ronda told herself this is what she had to do. Having no known history of breast cancer in her family did not take her risk away. It was a difficult time especially as she was going through stage 3 ovarian cancer. She had to train her mind to turn all negative thinking into positive thoughts, weighing up the pros and the cons, and the decision always came back to surgery.

She was given a year to think about it, in the meantime she needed to also stay focused on surviving her primary cancer and that alone was a huge call.

Once the year was up, Ronda had to get the go ahead from her oncologist who gladly referred her back to genetics for counselling. Her decision never once wavered. She didn't want to do this, but she had to do it for her family.

All she kept asking herself was, '*What If . . .*'

*What if* - she survived ovarian cancer and then developed breast cancer? Or *what if* - she had to fight two cancers at the same time?

*What If? What If? What If?*

Of course, Ronda did not want to die yet, she was only fifty-three, she had too much living to do. She wanted to see Lizzie and Bella marry, she wanted to be there for the grandchildren and at that present time, they only had Thomas who was still very little. She wanted to see them all start school, she wanted them to remember her as a fun-loving Grandma who she intended to be.

It's annoying when people keep telling you to be positive and you must fight the cancer. Cancer rules, you have no say in it, if it gets you, it gets you and there is nothing you can do about it.

The second blow, was being turned down for breast surgery when they said they would review her situation in a year's time. Ronda felt as though the NHS had failed her yet again. First, they turned her down for an ultra sound, because they insisted, she didn't need one.

They would not even consider she may have ovarian cancer when she did, at fifty-two years of age, she proved them wrong.

Ronda was in actual fact growing a cancerous tumor the size of a small melon, which was graded a four, this indicated her cancer was aggressive. This was not good news. If she hadn't kept throwing the toys out of her pram it would have cost Ronda her life.

Then there were the constant warnings from Little Acorns. But she could hardly tell anyone about them or they would have listed her as a basket case.
And then THIS . . .

It felt like a great big hammer had struck her on the head, while she had another melt down and trust me, she had one or two of those. She waited another long year before her case was reviewed.

In the meantime, she needed to have another mammogram at the breast clinic, the screening picked up a cluster of cells that represented cancer.
The following week Ronda was back in the breast clinic to have these suspicious cells drilled out under a local anesthetic.

For you ladies who are already of an age to have a mammogram, imagine laying on your side on the very edge of a treatment bed with severe fibromyalgia while the mammogram machine is pulled down to your chest, your breast is clamped in tight and squeezed while you are told you must lay as still as you can be, for over forty minutes while they drill into your breast.

Ronda was told to keep her eyes closed, but she opened them by accident and nearly passed out. There were tubes running to and from the breast filling with blood and grunge. The nurse explained they were drilling the cells and sucking them back out through the tube. Lovely!

The good news was these cells were nothing more than a cluster of calcium.

Maybe this made the panel stop and think 'it could have quite easily have been cancer' and then they would have failed her once again. Suddenly, they were keen to offer Ronda the bilateral mastectomy.

It still had to be discussed at another MDT meeting, and it was left to one surgeon who had the final vote and SHE said YES!

*This was really happening . . .*

Ronda was referred to a plastic surgeon to chat about the reconstruction. Thankfully she passed as a good candidate, you wouldn't believe the criteria you need to pass for complete double reconstructions.

The wait for surgery all seemed to happen rather quickly considering they needed an eight-hour theatre slot and two surgeons who both had their own full theatre medical team. It involved over thirty members of medics.

Again, she had the surgery at Addenbrookes Hospital in Cambridge. It was one hell of an operation but it all went very well.

She had lots of ongoing appointments back to the plastic surgeon's clinic. The implants he had given her were what are known as expanders. This means they gradually add saline to increase the size, so you are stretched gradually. The great side about this is you can keep going until you say stop, in other words you can go as large as you want and if you decide they are too big they can drain some of the saline out decreasing the size until you feel 100% happy.

How they do this is by inserting a tube from the implant to a little button, known as a port, about two inches down from your chest. The saline is past into this metal port by a long needle and syringe.

It was supposed to be a painless procedure, Ronda however, found it to be flipping agony. But that was only because they put pressure on her fibromyalgia rib cage, which basically felt like her ribs were broken if touched more than a tickle. No one else had this problem, so she insisted they must continue.

It got to the point she was begging them to take the implants out, she was prepared to go flat chested, the discomfort was too terrible to bear any long.

*'Ronda had, had enough.'*

It turned out she had developed severe capsular contractor, which is basically severe scar tissue that had grown over the implant during the healing process. Her surgeon wasn't about to give up on her though, he suggested they change the expanders for a different type of implant, they were more expensive, but they had a different outer coating and they helped prevent the same thing happening again.

Not everyone has problems with expanders, but if you are offered them and you are sure about your bra size, to prevent a second operation ask for the permanent ones. It prevents being black and blue after having the ports topped up.

Ronda was warned it could happen again, but they were exchanged and are still fine after ten or more years, and they continue to look amazing.

She stayed in remission from the cancer for eight amazing years, in spite of the many challenges, it all turned out well for her and she never once regretted her decision.

Both girls were young and Lizzie wanted another baby, Bella had just conceived her first child so she couldn't do anything until after the birth, however, she wanted more than one child. Even though it could be difficult, she had already gone through fertility treatment to conceive this baby and she wasn't getting any younger.

Of course, once you pass a life-threatening gene onto your children, you go through the guilt process. Then there was the survival guilt that constantly played on her life, her brother now gone, some very dear friends too. The anxieties you hold dear in your heart are in a way much harder to deal with than being diagnosed yourself.

When you think nothing could get any worse it does and it continues to do so. Your biggest fear becomes more than a bad dream, it turns into a real living hell.

Many folk wonder how people cope so well, it's strange how they do, they do because they have no choice, in spite of the many times Ronda and her family fell apart they always managed to pick themselves up.

Some days Ronda struggled to come to terms with the saying, 'What doesn't kill us, makes us stronger,' She didn't always feel as strong as everyone thought.

But while in remission she had to believe in the wonders of the NHS and believe this wasn't going to be the death of her, she was going to beat this – or was determined to try!

# Chapter 15

## 'GERD and Laden with Shopping'

Ronda had been feeling really bloated with significant digestive problems and was visiting the loo more often. She also had a great deal of chronic abdominal discomfort in her upper and lower digestive tract.

Her consultant sent her for a gastroscopy which diagnosed a hiatus hernia and severe esophagitis with an over lapping condition known as GERD, gastrointestinal reflux disease.

The inflammation was so severe she was borderline surgery. After all she had been through, she was relieved it wasn't cancer but shocked it was anything else. Luckily it was treatable and she was immediately prescribed with a drug known as Omeprazole to relieve the symptoms of gastrointestinal reflux.

In spite of everything that Ronda had been through on her first part of her cancer journey, she was made of strong stuff and she was starting to see her never ending trips to the hospital as a day's outing. It gave her a reason to dress up. Ronda came to the conclusion, the only way they could get through the cancer was by leading as normal a life as possible in between the hospital days and the horrendous chemotherapy side effects.

As if fibro fog wasn't bad enough, chemo brain offered a double type of whammy - No one could ever possibly imagine. The profound fatigue hit an unreal level of cognitive behavioural problems.

On one of her better days when Ronda decided she was pretty okay-ish to have a normal-ish day shopping, she ventured off into the town centre. She was just about ready to head off home when the fatigue once again came over her in a debilitating wave of exhaustion. But she had a couple more jobs to do on the way back to the parked car.

Laden with shopping bags Ronda made her way to the photographer's studio to collect the wedding photos she had ordered of her daughter's wedding.

First of all, Ronda had a huge problem with the fact that 'Jason' was called 'Julian' - and she proceeded to always call him Jason, which Julian found humorous.

As if that wasn't bad enough, she made an even bigger fool of herself when she found herself asking Jason/Julian what the date was so she could fill in the cheque.

His answer was something like, 'The 22$^{nd}$'

She wrote the twenty-two, forward slash and waited for further instructions.

As he looked her in the eye Julian giggled and said, 'You want me to tell you the month?'

'Well, yes,' she said without breaking into a smile - after a long silent pause, 'AND?' she said.

'AND?'

'Well, the rest please.'

'The REST?'

'Yes,' she scoffed, he really was making this harder

than it needed to be.

'Just tell me the flipping date' she chided.

Julian laughed so much - but all Ronda wanted to do was go home and cry. However, Ronda did what she always does and made light of her brain freeze with a chuckle and left the studio, with Julian well amused.

Ronda shuffled across the road to the South Holland Car Park to buy a yard brush from Wilkie's. She was fed up asking Billy to get one, he didn't see the need but the one they had was too big and heavy for Ronda to manage.

Now she really was about to collapse on her feet, but when she opened the car boot to dump the shopping bags inside, she struggled with the yard brush so decided it would have to go across the back seat. As soon as she had closed the boot, she realized what she had done.

In the struggle, Ronda had also locked her handbag in the boot with the car keys inside.

With no mobile phone, Ronda made her way to the hairdressing salon where her daughter worked along the Winsover Road. She knew Lizzie's boss well enough to ask if she could phone home.

The house phone was engaged, Billy would be at home but he would be using the telephone line to download his jobs of the day. That was the only internet connection they had back then.

Forty minutes later, Ronda finally managed to hear a ring tone and Billy picked up. He wasn't in the best of moods. He had already had a harrowing day and was hot under the collar with stress.

'For fuck's sake Ronda, what do you expect me to do about it?'

Pause . . .

'Well, can you meet me at the car park with the spare fob?'

'What spare fob? We don't have a spare fob.'

'What do you mean we don`t have a spare fob, of course we have a spare fob, it's on the key hooks in the kitchen.' She told him as she could picture it hanging there.

'Not for this car we don't, that's an old key from the old car.'

With that the line went dead and Ronda had lost the dial tone.

Eventually Billy called back, he had phoned the garage who luckily had the car details from when we bought the car from them, so they were able to cut another key. The fob would take a few days but although they could not drive the car without a fob, they could unlock the boot with the key and retrieve the fob from Ronda's hand bag.

The only other problem was the wait. Ronda needed to get back to the car soon to slap a note on the window screen for the car park attendant to explain what had happened, otherwise she would be blessed with a parking fine as well.

On the walk back Ronda spotted Billy's BT van at the traffic lights, she had never been so happy to see him. Sadly, the feeling wasn't mutual and he drove straight past her, making sure she walked all the way back to the car park.

Ronda was at breaking point her relief on seeing him turned into justifiable hate.

She was so exhausted and pained she had no idea how she could put one foot in front of the other.

Still holding nothing more than a yard brush which just looked daft, she realized Billy had no idea where exactly his wife had parked the car, it was also a big car park.

So she hid out of view forgetting about the yard brush sticking high above all the parked cars. As she watched Billy`s BT van slowly driving around the car park little did she know he was heading towards the yard brush.

In no time at all Billy had the boot of their car open and then he spotted the fashion stores shopping bags. She had been bubbled, and her plan to sneak into the house to hide her over indulgence from the clothing shops before he came home from work had been shattered, and now he knew!

He never stayed cross for long - and later he saw the funny side. He said he was just starting to feel sorry for her because he thought, 'Poor old girl, she isn't well and doing the weekly supermarket shopping on her lonesome.' That was before he realized she had spent all the housekeeping on a jolly.

The good news is . . .

*'A few years later he is still laughing about it!'*

# Chapter 16

## The Highway Code

No one warns you how cancer takes away your self-esteem, leaving little energy to do things to help yourself. Just as Ronda found a little confidence to get back behind the wheel of her blue Focus, she reversed successfully out of the drive onto the private block paved road that ran parallel to the Vernatts drain. Her nail appointment was for eleven am, she left in plenty of time allowing stopping time for the rail way line and the four sets of traffic lights into town. As she forgot to steer around the slight turn opposite her next-door neighbour's front door, she drove smack into the curb, splitting her tyre and crushing her alloy.

Not an excellent start to her first drive out alone since her last chemotherapy treatment. It could happen to anyone though, right? It just so happened it usually only ever seemed to happen to Ronda.

The last of mishaps with wrong car parks or wrong cars; locked keys in the boot; forgetting how to drive; trying to get out of the car with safety belt still fastened is pretty high. Of course, if you have already read Ronda's stories from Back in the Day, you will be aware how she failed her first driving test – miserably!

The point is, she should never be allowed in the driver's seat and now she is hectoring her Billy for her own car, as if owning her own set of wheels is ever going to change the fact she really is not safe . . .

I can hear what you are all thinking, surely, she can`t be that bad, trust me she has first class experience when it comes to 'A little accident . . .'

Now, don`t get me wrong, she is not one of these little grannies who sit tight against the steering wheel, even though she does have short legs. She certainly does not lean forward in her seat; bent over like she has an old age back condition. She does not clutch the steering wheel with white knuckles at five to one. She does not break at every slight bend in the road, she puts her foot on the gas and drives the car round.

She does not use the clutch to slow down, she feathers the brakes and goes through the gears.

Her highway code is 'A' star but that doesn't prevent little accidents. The fact that the wind blew an open gate onto the side of her yellow Vauxhall Chevette in the 1980's was hardly her fault. But it was a little accident and it cost Billy dearly to re-place the damaged door, wing and front bumper. In fact, that time the car was close to a right off.

Neither was it her fault when it rained so hard and the window wipers couldn't cope on the way to the baby clinic. Her vision was so incredibly distorted by the rain, she managed a head on collision into the two-foot-high wall outside the clinic's main entrance.

Ronda's brain doesn't seem to be wired the same as anyone else's. Most normal folk would at least get out of the car to check the damage. All Ronda was concerned about was how she was going to get from car to clinic door without getting her hair wet. Her mum used to tell her, 'It's too ruddy late once the horse has bolted,' unfortunately Ronda bore the same attitude.

A dozen pairs of eyes looked out of the window when they heard the crash, Ronda quickly grabbed her baby, who was sleeping in her baby seat in the rear of the car, and made a run for it.

'Are you alright my dear?' one of the health visitors asked kindly.

'Yes, we are fine thank you. Are you?' Ronda asked back, totally unperturbed by her little accident.

'And the car?' another asked.

'I dun know,' She shrugged as though she didn't give a fig. 'I will check when the rain stops, I'm sure its fixable,' She wasn't the least bit perturbed about how much their insurance claims were going to hit the roof after so many claims.

. . .

Beep, Beep, Beep - Ronda honked the horn, While Sheila locked her front door - taking her time from door to car.

'Hurry up Missis, we'll be late!' Ronda yelled. Honestly if she went any slower, she would fall asleep standing up.

It was a beautiful warm summers evening and such a joy to be driving to their dance class in the town centre, with the roof down. With their honey blonde bobs and dark sunglasses, they looked like the cousins had been cloned.

Now, folk may say having a love affair in one's late

fifties, has to be a midlife crisis. Ronda and Sheila's love affair with music, simply led them to where they felt comfortable, which was the 'Dance Floor,' and they were bloody good at it too.

Most people from their youth were crazy about northern soul. And it's true, once the music and dance get under your skin, it's difficult to let go and the 'all-nighter's' simply never stop after your teens.

But Ronda and Sheila where still in love with jiving . . .

The cousins had been through a lot together over the years. Sheila was four years older than Ronda, so they didn't really hang out together while growing up. However, when Ronda found out she was pregnant with her first daughter, Sheila announced that she was expecting her second child. The two infants were born within four weeks of one another. So Sheila and Ronda went through pregnancy classes together on a clinic day. Sheila was a great support with it being Ronda's first child and the fact she had no mum.

The two young mums met every Wednesday, one week Sheila would walk to Ronda's, the following week, Ronda would walk to Sheila's and they did this until the little girls started play group together. Two years later the children started school and they were inseparable for their primary school years. In their teens they went their separate ways, as they made lots of new friends at the secondary modern all-girls' school. Then they worked together for a while at the best hairdressing salon in the town, they trained with the same guy Ronda had all those years ago, and Ronda beamed with pride.

As life styles changed over the years and as time passes in the blink of an eye, it had been some time since Ronda and Sheila had done anything together UNTIL the two cousins were both diagnosed with cancer. Sheila's was in her breast, Ronda's her ovaries. The two women went through the devastating effects of chemotherapy at the same time, alongside bald heads and wigs, and many a teary eye.

Putting the reality aside, the ladies headed into town all dolled up to have their love affair with John Travolta. They wore the identical wigs but nobody would know, if it wasn`t for the fact Sheila was a lot taller than Ronda they could have been passed as twins.

Dance night always fell on a Monday evening. The council had already set out the frame work for the market stalls ready for the following morning. They took up the first parking space on the edge of the road leading into Red Lion Street. The old Red Lion pub was always oozing with drinkers even on a week night.

Now because Ronda wasn't confident about reversing into the parking spaces from the road, she indicated to turn right into Red Lion Street and attempted to drive round the market stall frames and forward into the next available parking space. It wasn't even a tight squeeze there was plenty of room to manaeuvre forward into the space, at least then she didn't need to reverse at all, not in or out.

Now, one of the downfalls with Ronda's driving skills is the fact she concentrates too hard on one thing at a time, she was totally oblivious of the massive concrete pillars supporting the storm porch that overhung the entrance door to the pub.

Bang!

'What the fuck, just happened?' as Sheila's head hit the window screen in front of her. Her wig shot forward and now her bangs were down to her chin.

Unfortunately for Ronda, her wig now sat in her lap.

'Oh dear,' Sheila said in a worried tone, 'the car.'

'Never mind the bloody car, what about our bloody dignity?' Ronda scoffed!

'Oh no,' Sheila said, 'look at the window,' as a dozen pairs of eyes stared out!

In a split second all hell was let loose by the guys who owned the set of eyes from the pub's windows.

Sheila was quickly straightening her wig, while Ronda reached for her bag to apply a little more lippy, totally forgetting about her now bald head. And there the pair sat, as if butter wouldn't melt.

'Do you ladies need any help?' one chap asked.

'I think they might, look at the bumper,' another said.

'Are you okay?' another asked, while the questions and banter continued.

All Sheila could say was, 'My head hurts,' and all Ronda could do was sit and laugh hysterically when she realized her wig now sat on her lap!

'Righty-o, darlings we need to get this car off the pillar,'

Ronda put it in reverse but all the car did was offer a crunching sound.

'Whoa, whoa, whoa - we need to pull the wing off the wheel,'

As a couple of guys, started to pull the wing out, the car rocked from side to side, backwards and forwards.

'Can yaw put the hand brake on luv,' the strong bloke with the tattoos asked.

'Mi head hurts,' Sheila groaned.

'I`m surprised you got back in the car with `er darling, are you sure she`s passed her test?' one of the guy's asked laughing.

'Oh, mi head,' Sheila groaned again.

'Are you alright luv, maybe someone should take you to the hospital to get that bump checked over.'

Once the car was moveable, Ronda got out to check the damage again. 'Oh, that looks so much better, I bet Billy won`t even notice.'

'Oh, lordy, lordy, lordy - what was Billy going to say?'

'Who the fuck is Billy?' one guy asked.

'Mi husband,' Ronda said.

'Well, I think he`ll notice darling,' the same guy laughed loudly.

'For fuck's sake, are you for real?' he asked Ronda jokingly.

All Ronda could do was laugh adding, 'He is going to kill me.'

'For someone who`s about to be killed you sure have a funny sense of fucking humour,' he chuckled.

'Eddi, stop with the swearing man, these ladies don`t need to be hearing it.'

'I think she`ll hear plenty more when her old man sees the state of his car.'

'Come on let's get this car parked up properly.'

'Oh, thank you so much, you are so kind.'

'Oh no luv, we ain't parking the car, you are.'

Ronda looked terrified, 'It's ok darling, we'll direct you. Just remember - SLOWLY!'

As the guys instructed her - Ronda reversed a little *'STOP!'* they shouted in unison before she reversed into the steel frames of the market stalls. She meant to drive forward slowly but the smooth soles of her dancing pumps slipped on the gas and she went a tad too fast. *'STOP!'* but it was too late!

Ronda seemed to bounce off the concrete pillars for a second time, but this time she had shattered the radiator. As steam oozed from under the bonnet in an opaque cloud, Sheila sat groaning at the side of her cousin as she bashed her head for the second time that evening.

'Oh, for fuck's sake, this is unbelievable,' someone chided.

'Yer, a good story for the Spalding Guardian,' another joked.

'How much do ya think, they'd pay us?' the same voice chuckled.

'Oh, mi head hurts,' Sheila complained for the hundredth time that evening, but all Ronda could do was giggle like a silly little thing just out of her gym slip.

*'This must have been the worst little accident Ronda had ever had and she is still laughing about it, but just in case you're wondering, Billy went ballistic, but he has mellowed in his mature years and they live to tell the tale.'*

# Chapter 17

## Here Again
## 2019

Life can pass by in a blink of an eye - never quite knowing what we are about to face.

Happiness and health can suddenly change leaving us devastated beyond oblivion.

A new nightmare began for Ronda in October 2018. Ronda and Billy's doctor was about to retire and they had no choice but to find themselves a new G.P. So they registered themselves with another locally run practice just around the time Ronda was due for her six monthly CA 125 blood test which was her ovarian cancer marker test. At the time Ronda was experiencing a little back pain but she put it down to her fibromyalgia, she wasn't worried but the blood test would put any unease to rest if the results were normal, and they were indeed normal.

Now, in spite of all Ronda's health issues she wasn't one to visit the doctor with trivial things like some folk do. To her that would be simply wasting a doctor's time.

The good thing about the new practice was you could a) order your meds on line, b) you could request a telephone appointment to save the bother of taking up a full appointment and, c) there were telephone options for all kinds of things, so that when you called in you always spoke to the right person.

It was the end of January 2019 before Ronda decided it was time to take a visit to see her new G.P. Over the Christmas and New Year, the pain in Ronda's right hip became intolerable, even on the strongest of pain meds. The pain was sending spasms through the lower right-hand side of her back and the sciatica pain down her leg and ankle worsened by the day.

Ronda began to worry this was more sinister than the aftermath of decorating the Christmas trees. It wasn't unusual for such tasks to flare up her fibromyalgia, but she had a gut feeling about this just as she had before.

It wasn't a matter of if her cancer came back, it was a matter of when. Ronda had no idea how she knew, she just did.

Ronda and Billy had no idea how they coped on top of all they had endured. This was a totally new level of hell.

Life was like a game of cards, it wasn't so much the cards that were dealt, but how they chose to play them...

But first she took the telephone option to speak to someone. Ronda briefly explained her concerns. Although she was fully aware it was sciatica pain that she was experiencing, she was concerned about what was causing it.

The G.P she spoke to took Ronda's past history into consideration and decided she needed an urgent appointment right away. Ronda was offered an appointment later that day at six forty-five pm, on 31st

January, Billy's birthday.

The GP was a very sweet lady doctor, but Ronda felt as though she wasn't taking her seriously. She confirmed that the pain Ronda was experiencing was indeed Sciatica, but when Ronda offered her concerns about the cause of such pain, the young pretty doctor shrugged and suggested it was very likely to be arthritis in the hip, and said she would send her for an x-ray. The doctor refused to offer any pain medication because of Ronda's diseased aesophagus. She suggested continuing with paracetamol, even though Ronda had already told her she may as well be taking Smarties.

Ronda went for her x-ray the following day which was a complete waste of time. The results were clear - no sign of arthritis. And the slight thinning of the bones, which was picked up eight years previously, appeared to have healed. Most odd!!

Ronda waited a few more days and again asked for a telephone appointment to discuss these results alongside her own concerns with fresh ears. By this time the sciatica pain was easing up but Ronda was experiencing a lot of pelvic pain, such as spasms and a stabbing shooting pain that doubled her over. The doctor she spoke to suggested she should be seen immediately and another appointment was made for later that day.

This time Ronda was seen by the doctor she was actually registered with. The date was 11th February, 2019.

As advised, she took a water sample with her, the results for that were also normal, so why did she have such excruciating pain in her bladder?

First of all, Ronda's doctor told her a sciatica nerve pain can take up to 16 weeks before it starts to get better, she had had this since October, and only now was it easing up but it had been taken over by a much more concerning pain.

The doctor asked a lot of questions about Ronda's cancer history and surgery before examining her. He examined her thoroughly asking if she experienced any pain while he poked and prodded her belly. There was no pain, but then suddenly came an almighty great big O…Ouch!

Once Ronda and the doctor were back in the consultation chairs, he twiddled his thumbs deep in thought before breaking the news.

'I will refer you for an emergency ultra sound scan at the Johnson Hospital.'
    There followed an almighty blow as he told her, 'I can feel a huge mass in your pelvis and it's pressing on your sciatica nerve and bladder.'

This was not what Ronda expected to hear from her G.P. Previously, her doctor eight years ago, didn`t even get out of her chair to examine her, let alone make a diagnosis.

Ronda insisted having her scan at Peterborough City

Hospital after the events concerning her referral eight years previously. After some hesitation the doctor agreed and switched the referral from Lincolnshire to Cambridgeshire.

When Ronda opened the car door to join Billy who was waiting in the car park, she was too choked to speak. How could she share this diagnosis when she had little time to process it herself?

Some of you may not be aware it's the patient's choice to which hospital you are sent. So bear that in mind for the future.

Two days later Ronda received an appointment in the post for the wrong hospital, the hospital she refused to go to, and, it wasn't until the 26th February. If that was supposed to be an emergency appointment, so help her God!

Ronda contacted the referrals department at the doctor's surgery, a recorded voice came on line 'You are fourteenth in the queue.'

After a long wait, and finally the next in the queue, Ronda explained her situation and explained her reasons why she requested that appointment to be cancelled, and a new referral made to the hospital Ronda had initially requested. After all she did have a massive notice slapped on her history records saying 'Do not send this patient to Lincolnshire Hospitals.'

The secretary was very honest by admitting it was her mistake that Ronda had been referred to the wrong hospital. She explained that even though the doctor had made a note not to send Ronda to the hospital in question, she took it upon herself to ignore it because, at that time the out of county hospital could not offer an appointment date. They told her it would be within two weeks. The secretary misunderstood, she thought, that meant it would be within two weeks to be given an appointment date. What they really meant was that Ronda would be seen within two weeks. It all sounds very complicated and who needs such stress on top of everything else.

The follow day, the city hospital gave Ronda a call offering her a scan later that same day.

Mr. Mooshe, the top consultant radiologist, did two ultra sound scans, one was the jelly on the belly, like you have when you're pregnant, the second was an internal scan.

He was very kind and insisted Ronda hadn't been looked after very well over the past three years. He asked WHY she hadn't had a scan in almost eight years?

Mr. Moshe confirmed that her GP was correct, there was indeed a large solid mass protruding from her pelvis and it was sitting right on her bladder and sciatica nerve, stating this explained the sciatica and bladder pain.

Mr. Moshe sent the results from the ultra sound scan immediately to her GP instructing him to refer her straight away for an urgent CT scan.

Ronda was back at the city hospital five days later for the CT scan.

The scan was booked for one hour later than her appointment time, this allowed preparation time. A cannula was fitted so they could insert a dye to show things up a bit better and then she had one litre of liquid to drink and hold in her bladder until she was called through for the scan. She was having a scan on her pelvis, abdomen and chest. The liquid wasn't the usual water that tasted like aniseed, which is vile, this time it looked like milk, had the same texture as milk, but it tasted of oranges. It was actually quite nice and much easier to swallow.

But that wasn't the problem, the problem was this large solid mass squashing her bladder. The pain built up very quickly until it became an overbearing, agonizing pain she could bear no longer.

Ronda had been early for her appointment by around thirty minutes, so this meant the fluid was to be held in her bladder thirty minutes longer than the usual hour. Then the scanner ran another forty minutes late, holding her bladder for two hours and ten minutes was not an option, or at least not with a whopping fifteen cm X eight point five cm solid mass sitting on her bladder, by this time she was close to tears.

Billy went to have a word with the nurse in charge.

Now after insisting she had to hold this fluid for an hour before her scan, she told the nurse what her problem was and she was sent to the loo immediately. Ronda asked if it would affect the scan and she told her it would be okay, it was more important that the liquid lined the cavity to get a clearer picture. So, why make patients so uncomfortable if it didn't really matter?

When the dye is put through you start to burn up, gradually it starts in the throat, then the belly and then right down into your pelvic floor. Most people insist they are peeing themselves especially on a full bladder, but Ronda found the warm sensation soothing as it eased her pain.

The following day, the results went to the MDT meeting where the consultants decide on the next step forward, in Ronda's case an immediate referral back to see her oncologist to discuss a treatment plan.

So it all happened rather quickly once she had been accepted at the right hospital. They had wasted around three weeks with the GP but that wasn't his fault.

The following day the GP phoned Ronda for a chat and he printed out the report ready for her to collect.

**This was the report:**
This lady has a large mixed echo mass arising out of the pelvis, the mass is largely solid measuring 15cm by 8.5cm.

With a right prominence urethra, the bladder seems to be involved. The mass displaces and compresses on the sigmoid colon which is not seen clearly separately to the mass.

In other words, they had no idea if the cancer had

spread into the bladder or colon but it could look that way.

The good news is - there were no ascites seen and the scan had no significant nodes.

Paralysed by her thoughts, Ronda managed the ordeal of the cancer's return.

'So, they are were going to operate, they told her, 'there is no evidence that it would change the outcome.' In other words, in time, she was going to die from this.'

. . . .

'Well, the bugger isn't getting me yet! I have too much living to do,' she thought with anger, but that didn't stop her from going into an overdrive of panic.'

Ronda decided that one of the first things she needed to do was write her own eulogy, she wouldn't want to put Billy and the girls through that.

She needed to plan the service; She wasn't even sure if that was even possible. And she was sure a church wouldn't agree on playing 'Super Girl' as her goodbye song!

So okay, they can't operate this time, they can only offer palliative intent, which basically means TREAT IT, so, she knew she would be hairless again by the spring – Such joys, well actually it isn't all as bad as you think, so don't go feeling sorry for me. Just be glad, I won't need to wax, shave, pluck, or epilate anything for a whole 6 months.

The not so good news is, WIGS are going to be too hot to wear all through the summer. So, it's either go bald or wear a scarf which could be just as hot as the wigs.

Ronda had prepared herself for nine cycles of chemotherapy with a gap of four weeks in between. At least this time she had an extra week to recover, although that could also mean it was because she would need it. She didn't dare ask!'

It's pretty much the same old, same old, they will be closely looking after her with blood tests, blood tests and more flipping blood tests. Luckily, they didn't phase her at all. As far as Ronda was concerned they could do what they needed to do to give her more time.

. . . .

Medical science had developed at a rapid rate since Ronda's first diagnosis. There was now an even stronger more effective chemotherapy available for Ronda's type of cancer called 'Caelyx,' another toxic drug derived from bacteria found in the soil. The oncologist described it as the RED DEVIL. And that description was not misnamed, it sure was about as evil as it could get, and Ronda was at risk of going into epileptic shock.

*'Dear God, I am not ready to die, not yet'*

Paranoia became hysteria, and the battle continued for some time before it got any easier. Ronda, persevered and fought on, refusing to give up hope in surviving her dreadful plight. She found the six months of chemotherapy too gruesome to ever go through it again. 'NO,' she said 'I`m done with chemo.' Ronda was wiped out by the long list of never-ending symptoms.

Nearing the finishing line Ronda had another CT scan. The scan revealed the platinum-based chemo had been a success, the tumour had been destroyed by a whopping 95%. The remainder measured the size of a small chicken's egg. Her oncologists decided to save the final three rounds of chemo to be used at a later date.

This news was brilliant because it meant that Ronda now qualified to go forward with targeted therapy. A Parp Inhibitor prevents further mutation by blocking cancerous cells.

After six months of targeted therapy, the follow up CT scan suggested the Parp inhibitor had stabilized the tumor.

Ronda's indomitably, optimistic mind, was beginning to feel that she might just survive this ordeal a while longer.

*The world is where most things happen to us. The brain is where we process stuff.*
*To think positively about a negative situation is foolish.*
*To think negatively and irrationally about the situation would be unhealthy.*
*To think negatively and rationally was the wisest and healthiest option.*

The following scan was delayed because of the covid pandemic and seven months later the tumour had grown at a rapid rate and she was taken off the drug.

All Ronda's hopes had been pulled from under her.

The thing is Ronda felt so incredibly well on the Parp. The only side effects were all good, she lost weight without even trying, her hair grew back after the second chemo hair loss. She felt sexy, full of life and energy. All of her fibromyalgia and chronic fatigue symptoms had waned, she ran everywhere bragging, and the only thing that was getting in the way of life now was Covid-flipping-19.

Ronda continued to struggle with the fact Niraparib didn`t work for her, or not in the way it was expected to. Emotionally it left her broken. With no delays the oncologist put her right back on chemo.

Ronda had spent almost two years on continuous cancer treatment with no break and it had left her exhausted beyond repair.

The stress of illness and the fears of covid 19, added to Ronda's anxiety levels and mental wellbeing, taking its toll. She was now on the Critical Extremely Vulnerable list. This meant she would be less likely to survive should she be floored with the deadly virus.

Ronda was pretty much isolated for that year. However, while she remained focused on the chemo, she was able to put the Covid situation to one side, because either way she needed to be in isolation. Her writing and other hobbies kept her occupied through until September 2020 when she went back on the chemotherapy and then life became really tough again and she struggled, really struggled.

She wanted to stop the treatment - but her doctors voice kept ringing loudly in her ears. When Ronda asked the question, she told her she had one to two years life expectancy with treatment, Six months to a year without treatment.

She had just completed six cycles of carboplatin and pacitaxol and was waiting for her end of treatment scan on 1st February, 2021.
Now it greatly depended on her scan results.
And she had NEVER been so scared in her life.

**Ronda tells us:**

'I do know further treatment options may be possible, but right now I do not feel strong enough to go through anything else. I just want to get better and live a good life the best way I know how, for as long as possible.
'All this lost time is wasting time, it is taking away the time I should be spending with my family and friends.
'I know it's the same for everyone and that certainly does kind of make it easier, because I am isolated, but then so is everyone else. Some days I feel as though I am going mad, other days I feel blessed that I have so much me time to control my days without anyone else controlling them for me. What I can or can`t do, where I go, who I see.
'When you have a lot of wonderful friends and a

fabulous family, plans are often changed or broken, It hasn`t been like that through Covid.'

*'If I want to sleep the whole day, I can, I do!*
*If I want to just stay in my PJ`s to weed the garden, I can, I do!*
*I can leave the dusting for a month, go hairless, no makeup, just be a basic slob if that's what I want to be.'*

'In spite of being ill I have achieved so much more than most.

I spent 2020 in lock down but I succeeded on becoming a first-time author, I didn`t only write my first book, I had it published and it has been a great hit with my readers.

Something I would have never been able to achieve if Covid hadn`t happened at that precise time.

'I had finished all the crafting hobbies, by February 2021 I had made all my Christmas presents for those I care about.

'I made curtains and other home furnishings for our new home. I baked cakes, read books, painted, made masks, made Christmas decorations, I even had a bash at a diamond painting of my grandchildren, and succeeded with a resin painting too.

'I had dentist work done to give me a lovely smile. And so much more.

'Now, I just feel as though I am left dangling like a puppet on a string, collecting dust while I . . . Wait! Wait! Wait!'

# Chapter 18

## 1st February 2021

Bleep, bleep went the alarm clock at seven-thirty am.

Ronda, rolled over, pulling the duvet further around her chin. It was a chilly morning; snow had fallen and lay covering the bank and the landscape. Even the Vernatts had a slither of ice coating the river.

She stretched every tired, stiff muscle in her fibromyalgia body to prevent contraction from the cold morning she was about to face.

She left the shower running while she quickly made the bed. She was fastidious about how her bed was made, her mother had taught her the proper way, 'The Barkley way.'

'Get off Tabby,' she chastised the cat, Tabby didn`t budge, she settled down in a ball and peeped at Ronda over her paw, while Ronda made the bed around her.

'There, you can stay there until we get home,' she told her cat while she stroked her chin.

Mog had already settled on the bedroom chair, that's where he would be all day. While Kitty continued to fuss and meow around Billy`s legs as he proceeded to make the tea downstairs in the kitchen.

Ronda groaned with pleasure as she welcomed the hot jet from the power shower, in the small ensuite.

Daylight was breaking while Ronda dressed. The neighbours were leaving for work, which helped Billy and Ronda feel lucky with the fact they were now retired, in spite of the day ahead - indeed they felt lucky. It was a rare occasion when they relied on the bleeping of the alarm clock, getting up at the crack of dawn never did appeal to either of them, but now they usually had the pleasure of waking when they were ready.

Ronda was unsure why she should be anxious about today's appointment; she had been through this a dozen times before this day. It wasn't a painful procedure; it only gave slight discomfort and it was over pretty quickly anyway. It was the results that gave her the most anxiety, and holding one's bladder was about as bad as it got.

She wouldn't even be asked to take her clothes off. She remembered not to wear an under wired bra not that she ever needed to after her double mastectomy. With her good reconstruction she had no need to wear an undergarment at all, only to hide her permanently erect fake tattooed nipples. She removed any bling and remembered to wear leggings to avoid having to take off her jeans with the metal button, so, basically all well prepped for the off.

'You've had several of these before haven't you,' the nurse asked kindly.
    'Yes, this one makes number twelve.'
    'Ah, bless, you know what to expect then.'
    'Sure do.'
    'Let's look at your veins, I expect you've have had a lot of cannulas too.'
    'Yup, but they tell me I`m juicy.'

'No stent then?'

'Not been necessary yet,' Ronda replied.

'I don't actually mind, I find them quite relaxing.'

'Do you?'

'The actual scan I mean.'

'Oh,' the nurse smiled.

'Well, the bed is comfortable and the pillows are so comfy I want to take one home with me,' she told the nurse with a chuckle.

'What about the dye?'

'Well, I quite like that too, I find it soothing, in fact I could easily nod off if the whole procedure took longer.'

The nurse giggled, 'I can see you're an easy patient.'

The really good news was the fact that protocol had now changed slightly, she only had 500 mls of liquid to drink instead of the usual one litre, and the waiting time had been reduced from an hour to thirty minutes.

The scanner started to rev like an aircraft getting ready for take-off. The treatment bed started to vibrate as the engine revved sounding more like a helicopter, as the propellers rotated faster and faster, the scanner machine became louder and louder. It settled down after take-off exactly how it did on any flight.

'Take a deep breath in,' the voice on the loud speaker instructed, 'and hold.'

Pause . . . 'Breathe normally.'

The polo mint, slowly moved a little further down the abdomen stopping again to voice further instructions.

'Deep breath in, and hold.' Pause . . . 'Breathe normally.'

'Okay Ronda, the dye is now being injected.'

While Ronda felt the heat sensation of the dye as it passed through the vein in her arm it flowed hotly to her throat and stayed there for a second before moving further down to her abdomen and lastly her pubic bone, she continued to follow the radiologist's instructions.

'Deep breath in, and hold.' Pause . . . 'Breathe normally.'

'ALL DONE!'

'What did you think to the hot flush?' the male nurse asked.

'Oh, this lady tells me she likes it,' the nurse told him.

'Really,' the young chap chuckled.

'I do indeed, I find it quite . . .' *pause* 'comforting,' she said with finality after she had given it some thought, which caused a bit of a giggle among the nursing staff.

Ten minutes in recovery, cannula out then home . . .

Well at least it was a day out! Now it`s the long wait for the results to come through.

Questions, questions, too many questions!

Has the chemo worked? – 'YES'
Has it killed the cancer? – 'NO'
Has it shrunk the cancer? – 'YES'

Has it stabilized the cancer? – 'DON'T KNOW'
How long in remission? 'Three months to three years,'
How long to next scan? – 'Six months'
What happens now? 'Watch and Wait.'
More treatment? – 'YES eventually'

# Chapter 19

## The Grim . . .

Ronda had a vivid memory of her mother thrashing her brother, especially the day she chased Neil around the dining room table with the horse whip while he squealed like a pink piggy at the Tuesday cattle market. Sometimes she had to pinch herself and ask 'Am I really this lucky.'

*'Indeed, I am . . .'*

Everyone dreads mentioning the 'C' word. It's a bit like Harry Potter and, *'He who must not be named'* And yet Harry Potter never thinks twice about saying 'LORD VOLDERMORT.' And Ronda knew if she didn't speak of the cancer soon, she'd be up shit street without a paddle.

Ronda had feared the unknown for most of her life, she had feared cancer, she saw it the only way she knew how: a Death Sentence.

But do you know what? With science research and the vast number of trials, they are always working hard to understand it more, they are experimenting on better treatments and they will never give up on finding a cure. The biggest battle is confronting the many different types of cancer, and as soon as they crack one, another new one is discovered, some ovarian tumours can grow as many as three different types of cancer in the one tumour, and they all need to be treated.

When Ronda`s own mum fought this devastating disease there was no ultra sound, CT or MRI scans. It is so important to donate, if we don't want to take part in the charity runs and all those other marvelous charity events that people are constantly doing, then we must sponsor the people who do.

Cancer effects all people one way or another, at any age, any race, gender or creed.

I think the scariest part of it is, it comes with no warning, one day you may be fine and the next you are experiencing your first symptom. Cancer creeps up on us often with no symptoms at all until it's too late, ovarian cancer is one of a few. There are thousands of people out there right now who have cancer, they just don`t not know it - yet.

We must never compare our own cancer with another, they are all unique in their own way. Treatments are individual too and most importantly the prognosis will be too.

The cause is most probably just as unique as the rest of the whole nasty business.

Cancer is clever it fools people. Often it fools our oncologists too, we go to get checked out for one thing and really it's something else. Often the root of the problem isn't picked up right away. We need to be self-aware, go with our gut feelings, talk it through with our GP. If they are not very interested it's our job to make sure they check us out and talk it through with us. If you are not happy, then request a second opinion.

Never take it for granted when all the tests come back

normal, unless you find out the root of the symptoms, we need to investigate deeper.

Cancer doesn't need to be a death sentence; even terminal patients live longer these days and it's only going to keep on improving.

Remember the Mcmillan and Mari Curie nurses who do a tremendous job supporting those who fight the disease. Imagine where the cancer world would be without them.

This is such a complex disease and I only know a small part of it, but I will do my very best to reassure you by sharing Ronda's story. And I hope that it may help a few of you. If one person's life is saved through her eyes then it's worth every second of my time writing this.

I know what I am going to say to you is easier said than done but try not to think negative thoughts. You can still be positive and realistic. Burying your head in the sand doesn't get things done and trust me, you mustn't do that whatever you do. Denial is the worst possible thing you can do. Cancer loves denial, that's how it survives best and destroys the most.

We are not only individual in the way we cope in a critical situation, but we may also cope differently from one day to the next, even from one short moment to the next. One minute we can think we are doing okay the next we can be having a bigger wobble than a two-year old.

We wouldn't be human if we didn't behave like that sometimes. We are allowed, we have a lot of the unknown to face up to. Even with the most accurate diagnosis in the world, it can often turn out different. Believe and trust in miracles, they do happen sometimes.

Whether it is you or a loved one with the cancer, don't sweat the small stuff, none of us can be sure of the ifs, buts, and maybes, until they do or do not happen.

Nothing is set in stone with these things. Feeling anxious is normal, but allowing negative thoughts that can take over your way of thinking is a massive waste of energy.

Each time you think 'What if . . .?'

Tell yourself, it may never happen. Deal with it when the 'what if' becomes a reality. Otherwise, you will make yourself ill. Ronda has leant this the hard way, and she should know. Whether we are the patient or the care giver, we need to stay strong to fight this demon. Ronda will tell you she had many a wobbly moment.

It's always difficult to know what to say to someone newly diagnosed with cancer, especially those who maybe facing the worst-case scenario.

You really only need to say a few words, it will mean a lot to know they are in your thoughts. Silence can create an atmosphere and it can make the patient feel terribly uncomfortable.

It's okay to ask questions but select them carefully. Some questions can be cruel. It's difficult to know if the patient really wants to talk about it or not. If they do, then they will. Be ready to listen.

It's okay to tell them they look well as long as it's meant in the right way, don't lie. Something's are best not said when it's not the right thing to say.

Don't be over positive, that has a two-way meaning.

Don't say ridiculous things like, 'I am so relieved to hear your voice because you sound no different.'

They may sound no different because they are no different, however reassuring that may be for you, that doesn't mean they are okay, it still means the patient has cancer and has a massive challenge ahead of them, they may be falling apart inside.

It's not alright to say something like, 'You can fight this, you did before,'

'You can do this darling,' would be a much softer approach, otherwise they may see such a comment as denial, and they need you to listen so they know they are being understood.

Most of the time they will be putting on a painted smile for your benefit, that doesn't mean they will welcome jokes and silly laughter. This could be misread as something else. If they want to make jokes about themselves and their plight – that's okay. And its also okay to chuckle with them.

The last thing they want to hear are stories about every other Tom, Dick and Harry who has or hasn't had cancer. They need you to listen to their own story.

Don't ask how they are, followed by issues that are happening in your life, that is not helpful. Remember, people with cancer are churned up by so many of their own problems, the last thing they want to hear is *YOUR* problems, this is not okay, even if they have always been there for *YOU* in the past, now it is the time for roles to be reversed.

Remember, ladies with cancer may wear makeup and make sure their hair is nicely styled, this hides a multitude of sins. So, chose your words carefully, when you tell them, 'You look so well,' because, looks can deceive and they may be feeling wretched, wait for them to tell you if they feel well or ask how they feel. It's okay to ask if they feel poorly? Or, 'I know you always look amazing but how are you feeling?' would be a better way of asking or, 'I know you always sound cheerful but how are you really.'

Wigs can often cause a stigma, someone may say 'I don't know why you bother,' this can be taken badly. If they chose to wear a wig and it's terrible, say nothing, if it looks fabulous tell them their hair looks nice, rather than, 'Your wig looks nice.' The later can come across as a deception of the truth. If it's a totally new look, tell them how you like the new colour or style.

Some ladies choose not to wear a wig and that's perfectly okay too, accept it as their individual choice, if their choice is different to what yours would be in their situation, to voice your opinion is not always going to be welcome.

Sometimes a wig can be far too uncomfortable, they can make you very hot, they can itch, or they can cause a head ache when wearing for long periods at a time. Should the wearer decide to take it off, don't scoff and tell them to put their bloody wig back on, just because it embarrasses you, don't expect them to wear it for your benefit, wigs are for their own benefit and no one else's so, respect that.

Long before Ronda's own diagnosis, she heard someone make a comment about a relative they had recently visited - 'You would have thought she would have put her bloody wig on, when she knew we were visiting.' Ronda never forgot those judgmental words, especially when he couldn't possibly have understood why that day she decided not to.

Don't tell them you don't like the short grey look while its growing or while they are waiting the six months after chemo before they can have it coloured, or tell them they didn't like it while it was growing because it was short and manly.

I have heard cancer patients say, they get more sympathy if they ditch the wig and the makeup. However, should we choose to do that in the comfort of our own home, it doesn't mean we are attention seeking when you pay them a visit. Some days they will feel rubbish and they may not have the energy to take care of their looks.

Some judge for looking too glamorous too, they seem to think we can't possibly be as ill as we say we are when we look so good, trust me - they can.

Imagine someone whose hair is their pride and joy and they have perhaps always worn it long and NOW they have none. The last thing they need is you complaining because the covid restrictions prevent you from getting your own hair done! Actually, Ronda couldn't resist saying a few times, 'Think yourself lucky, at least you have hair.' But, mostly she would tell them to 'Stop moaning, shave it off and wear a wig,' which usually stopped them complaining.

She confessed later, how mean that was when her own hair grew back and she was making the same complaint when they were in the second lockdown of Covid-19.

While she was going through cancer, an elderly relative told her, 'You don't want to get old, girl.'

She had listened to all his arthritic problems and humouring him as he showed her his long repeat prescription list. She could not resist telling him, 'Well, actually I do, want to get old.' She then removed her wig to remind him good and proper what she was going through, thirty years his junior.

'For Christ's sake put the fucking wig back on,' he said.

*It made her laugh out loud because he was a horrible man anyway, but that's because she was in a good frame of mind that day, and as far as she could see, he could only let himself down. However, another day, she would have reacted quite differently.*

Sometimes people can say the cruelest of things, sometimes they just say things without putting their brain into gear. Sometimes they don't ask, 'How are you doing?' Other times they are so disinterested, they brush it under the carpet, after all how can this be happening to a pretty young women who still looks beautiful. And sometimes they fear your answer so they change the subject and talk none stop about themselves.

Now don't get me wrong, it is important to talk about normal things, Ronda needed normal conversation too. It's all about the right balance, she would continue to listen to her friends and relatives, as long as they showed interest in what she was going through. But honestly, when people close their eyes to indicate they are well and truly not in the least bit interested in cancer, try doing the same when they talk none stop about their own problems. More often than not, their problems may be of the utmost priority to them but nothing can come close to a death sentence.

Don't turn every negative comment into a silly positive one, they will do that all by themselves, it doesn't mean they want to hear it from other people.

If someone told you - they felt ugly, would you agree? I dare say not.

When you have no idea what to say or fear saying the wrong thing, offer to make a cake, do some shopping, paint their nails, take in the ironing. One day it could be you in the need for support.

Never assume they have family who are doing those things, it doesn't mean they are, even if they should be. Tell them not to be afraid to ask for help. You could offer to take them for a hospital appointment, or sit with them so they are not alone. One of Ronda's best of friends sat with her two evenings a week, just so that her husband could continue to play darts. Things like that mean such a lot, she was quite happy to read the paper or magazine, while Ronda slept. That's what good friends do.

Having her first course of chemo gave her one good weekend out of four - another best friend made a point in taking her out for a meal when she felt well. That's what real friends do, they message you every single day, they are right by your side when you need it the most. It's the moral support that has the most effect and a huge difference on how to make progress, it also takes some of the strain away from close family members.

Imagine, if you have cancer, you are sat in the car looking like a glamour puss, with a good wig and dark shades, to hide more than the sun. You rummage through your bag in search for your disability parking badge. You have this strong overwhelming feeling that you are being watched. You notice an elderly couple sat in the car next to yours, they are talking, then turning heads towards you, then chatting some more, they look again while you slap your blue badge on the dashboard.

They are really staring now, obviously thinking you must be a fraud, they glance your way for the fifth time in the last three minutes. So how do you react? Maybe aggression or maybe you turn it into humor.

Ronda looked back with a big smile and pulled her wig off. The look left on their faces said it all . . . Of course, none of this is fun, far from it, but it greatly depends on how it is handled. Cancer doesn't come with a rule book, there are no rules, we make them up for ourselves as we go along.

**For those of you going through Cancer** - remember, we can take a little bit of control, Ronda shaved her blonde shoulder length bob off four times over a ten -

year period, that gave her a bit of control, cancer sucks, but she wasn`t going to let it take her pride and joy, that decision had to be all hers.

It felt like the most liberating thing she had ever done in her life. If you want to shout scream and throw a tantrum, then do it. Remember we cannot be brave all the time, it would not be humane to expect it from us.

### 'If we have cancer, it is a big deal.'

Of course, it always means a lot when people do offer, but it'll never be the people you expect and often it's the relatives that run the mile in the opposite direction, never assume the family is coping okay on their own, never assume they are doing as well as they seem to be, they will have their darkest of moments too.

Allow yourself to express your feelings and talk them through with your family, LOUD and CLEAR. If you are a *'want to know'* kind of person your oncologist will pick up on that, especially if you ask questions. They don't usually go into detail unless you ask. Not everyone wants to hear it.

It's important for us to be clear about what we want, but remember not everyone else will be in the same frame of mind.

Never forget the loved ones, they will need kindness too, never assume they have it under control, they will have days when they are at breaking point. Offer to do the difficult jobs like the ironing or cook a meal. Even if your friend/relative has only needed a lumpectomy with no follow up treatment, they may be still falling apart and trying to hold it together. Be kind, if you're not very good with words, show your concern by baking a cake.

Never say 'I'll be there for you.' unless you are sure you can follow it through. Be clear what you mean.

You learn a great deal about people when you go through something like this. A friend should be forever not someone who drops you the minute you get sick. Some may try to be over positive, it's because they fear the worst and they want to keep you strong, but that can also be really irritating.

'So, ask yourself, what is the worst-case scenario about 'The Grim?'

### *'We DIE'*

Well, we can't run away from the fact 'We are all going to die one day,' and if the grim doesn't get us something else will. Remember no one is immortal. Since her first round of cancer eleven years ago, Ronda had seen so many people she knew, and some she had loved dearly, who have fought the grim battle or lost their life to the evil beast that it is.

So, if you have a choice, ask yourself what would you prefer? if you could actually choose your destiny?

Would you choose old age and a nursing home, dementia or the aftermath of a stroke. Or would you choose a sudden accident?

Answer . . . 'Neither.' I thought not!

'So, what's so bad about THE GRIM?'

For many it's the knowing, for others it's the not

knowing, it can be liberating to have a certain amount of control, it gives us a little bit of time to prepare.

'By explaining, I hope this helps.'

Saying good bye is really hard and you cannot be strong for everyone else. But if it brings any comfort at all you can find a strength you could never imagine possible.

Ronda remembered the bitter cold of January, 2010, she was recovering from another round of chemo treatment, when she noticed the foreigners working in the field opposite her house, doing a tedious back aching job cropping cabbages one by one with their bare hands.

She stood at the window and wept for them, so there she was, not knowing if she would live or die and these poor souls frozen in their boots to make a small income.

She actually felt like the lucky one. She could stay in the warm comfort of her own home, financially secure, loved and comfortably numb.

The following day she watched a second world war film. It broke her heart to see the devastation the war did. 'Again, how could she complain?'

So, there is a lot to compare with the Grim. You may think this is the worst thing ever, but there are always people going through their own worst ever nightmare. It may be very different, it may be equally as sad and painful, but their fight is just different, that's all. It's JUST DIFFERENT!

Mentioning the `C` word really didn`t bother Ronda anymore, 'IT IS WHAT IT IS' but sometimes it's just 'GRIM.'

# Chapter 20

## 'Intimacy'

As days turned into weeks and weeks into months Ronda suffered several new challenges, both mentally and physically. She had periods when she felt almost normal and strong, especially compared to the many times her fibromyalgia and chronic fatigue syndrome had floored her over the years. But now it was hard to accept that the prognosis for her life expectancy could possibly be correct. It felt far too surreal, she found it hard to get her head around that. She couldn`t die from this . . . she had too much living to do.

Billy always seemed to understand when she needed physical contact, how important it was for her to draw strength from him. 'He raised her up' were the perfect words that captured everything he did for her. 'She could stand on mountains and walk on stormy seas,' Now, she had to be strong for him, he was too precious to ever let go, because he made her more than she could ever be, without him.

Her emotions brimmed each time she thought of how lucky she was to have so many people who cared.

Once her father told her, she was unlovable and now she would prove him wrong! Sometimes we need to be loved first before we can possibly know how to express it ourselves.

Now Ronda was only too familiar with support groups, but only as a chair leader, not like a sitter. Well, now she was about to find out how someone else`s group was organized. It was the hospital who put her onto it and like Ronda`s groups, the venue was at the hospital.

She didn`t know why she was feeling so nervous. More than she ever did chairing her own. This group ran weekly rather than monthly and each week the two hours get together would be split into a certain related topic and free chatting time among themselves.

This week's topic was personal issues about intimacy and lack of libido. This was something that could be really difficult for women to talk about openly, especially among the more mature age groups.

A lack of libido is not unusual in women who go through the menopause, with changing hormones running riot, these alone can offer a barrow load of problems but when they are fighting a cancer with the after math of body changing surgeries, they often lose body confidence, as their sexual identity is robbed from them and low self-esteem adds to the whole miserable depression of it. Of course, there are always other factors involved as well such as profound fatigue, pain and drug related side effects, the list can be long as the domino effect tumbles down on them.

And then . . . their hair falls out and they grow the dreaded beard.

Each woman will cope differently but often they just need to feel beautiful and sexy.

This could be interesting - thought Ronda as she carefully applied her luminous pink lipstick and pouted her lips in her Radley cosmetic mirror. A quick squirt of perfume and she was ready to face the world.

Ronda had arrived in good time, but not nearly enough to grab a coffee first. The group met in the oncology department, it would be interesting to know if the group was led by an ovarian cancer survivor, support groups are often chaired by someone who understands from the heart, because of their own personal related experiences.

Please dear God don`t let it have a circle of chairs, she had no idea why this way of seating made her nervous. Three other women were already seated with empty chairs left between them. Ronda sat at the nearest chair to the door, so she could make a quick exit if it all got too much. The other ladies smiled but none of them uttered a word, not to each other or to Ronda.

Ronda hated silence, it made her uncomfortable, so she broke the ice by asking if they had been before, two had, one hadn`t.

'That's good to know.' Ronda said, 'It can`t be all bad if you are here again.'

'Oh no, it isn`t,' the chubby middle aged blonde lady told her. 'We laugh, we cry, we laugh again,' she told her. 'My name is Valerie, by the way.'

'I`m Ronda,' she told all three women.

'And I`m Audrey, it`s my first time at one of these sessions.'

Audrey was clearly wearing a wig. It`s funny how everyone claimed no one would know it`s a wig, and Ronda could spot them quite easily, maybe because she had a wide experience with them, she had, after all, purchased a nice collection of eight over the past eleven years. Plus, the fact she had her own hairdressing business before she retired with ill health, may also have something to do with it.

The other lady sat chewing nervously on her finger nails. She wore a very pretty pink head scarf, that she had plaited and laid over the top of her head, knotting it for security on the opposite side.

Valerie, Audrey and Ronda sat with their heads turned towards her waiting for an introduction, but she chose not to speak.

'So, is this your first time?' Ronda decided to ask the nail chewer with the pretty braided pink head scarf.

'Second,' she said followed by a pause, before saying, 'I`m Carol.'

'It doesn`t look as though anyone else is coming,' Ronda said.

'I`m not at all surprised if we are going to talk about sex,' Valerie said.

'Well yes, I`d imagine some ladies might find it a little awkward,' Ronda offered.

'Humm,' Carol hummed quietly to herself.

Before anyone could get into the full swing of a conversation, the double doors flew open with a bang as they each bashed the wall to allow a rather large lady enter in a wheelchair. Her head was smooth and shiny from hair loss after her chemo. Her skin had a healthy-looking glow to it, her round chubby cheeks were naturally rosy and she greeted everyone with a perfect white smile.

'Ello you lot, for those who don`t know me already, my name is Sue.'

She mopped the sweat from her forehead with her sleeve. 'Bugger, it`s hot in `ere in it?' she chortled loudly.

'Yes, it`s a bit warm today dear, isn`t it,' Valerie agreed.

'Can one of you lot, open a window, before I pass out.' Sue chuckled.

Ronda didn't hesitate she was out of her seat opening the top windows with pleasure.

The door swung open again, another two ladies joined the group, followed by one of the Mcmillan nurses.

Ronda was already acquainted with Debbie. The other two ladies introduced themselves casually as Crissy and Sheila.

Eight ladies in total was a nice number. Sometimes too few can feel uncomfortable, too many can send the group in disarray, especially if they are all a bit gobby as the likes of Sue.

Debbie didn`t hesitate before starting, everyone seemed at ease, they all seemed quite a jolly bunch.

Carol was a little quiet but the others chatted freely.

'So,' Debbie started, 'how do you ladies feel about talking openly about intimacy?'

'Or the lack of it,' Sheila jested.

'Here, here, a cuddle would be nice,' Audrey added.

'My old man gets the wrong idea right away when I just want a cuddle so we never bovver wiv either,' Sheila scoffed.

'Well, my libido dropped when I turned forty, and it had nothing to do with cancer back then,' Audrey told them with certainty.

'Yes, a woman`s libido often drops with the onset of the menopause, there are several reasons to cause it but, today we are addressing lack of libido while living with cancer,' Debbie explained.

Carol raised her hand in the air . . .

'Yes, Carol,' Debbie acknowledged.

'When you say libido, do you mean sex?'

'Of course, she means sex, come on Carol, keep up old girl,' Audrey laughed.

'Come on Debs, tell us what you mean - if you mean sex say flipping sex!' Sue chortled with humour, while the others chuckled among themselves.

'So, who`s going to start?'

Of course, no one wanted to start so a long pause followed before Sue decided to enlighten the group on some of her sexual activities.

Audrey put her hand up in the air before she went on to share that she and her husband hadn`t made love for twelve years and now she wanted to try again, her husband was unapproachable. 'I just don`t know how,' she said with teary eyes.

'Just tell `im straight.' Sue told her, 'If ya want a shag tell `im ya want to shag,'

'Yes well, not everyone is as uncouth as you, Sue,' Crissy told her.

'Well, it sure `asn`t affected me and my old man, we still go dogging once a week and if I`m too knackered to be bothered, I do the watching, if ya know what I mean,' Sue laughed. Just as Valerie took a sip of sparkling water, she choked and spat it all over as the fizz ran out of her nose, her plain silk red blouse showed every mark from the soaking, while Sheila sat po-faced in disgust.

'Dogging?' Ronda and Audrey asked in unison.

'Oh please, don`t explain,' said Valerie, 'we really do not need to know,'

'Don`t knock it if you `aven`t tried it yourself,' Sue told them as though this was the norm these days.

'Well, it held me and my old man together through all this cancer shit,' she informed the other seven ladies.

Oh, my God, Deb`s face was a picture, she had no idea how to change the 'dogging' subject. Ronda knew she needed a bit of moral support, but she didn`t feel as though it was her place to step in. Instead, she couldn`t control her own giggling.

'How many of you ladies have had an affair then? Or your old man? Come on then, let's hear it?' Sue wanted to know. . .

'You mean before or after the cancer?' Crissy asked.

'Oh, please don`t encourage her,' Ronda laughed.

'No, it's a free country, let her ask,' Sue scoffed.

'It makes no difference Crissy my sweet, you're not being deceitful if you both participate.'

'How?' Crissy wanted to know.

'Oh please, spell it out to her somebody,' someone chided.

'No, no, please don`t,' Valerie begged.

Ronda continued to giggle, while Debbie sat with her jaw dropping further south.

'It`s like this,' Sue started. 'Dogging ain`t cheating, is it?'

'So, how does your husband participate?'

'I`m sure Sue doesn`t need to answer that ladies,' Debs said with caution.

'Tell us how this helped during your darkest days of cancer,' Ronda asked.

'Well, it's like this hun, life is too short, at least with a cancer diagnosis we have a bit of time to live the dream. To try all the things we have often wondered about. It can be going up in a hot air balloon, it can be para-gliding or bungee jumping, a race for life, a world cruise, pink hair - the list is long. We are all different, it depends what rocks your boat but usually once we have achieved something we will want to do it again. That's what dogging has been like for me and my old man. It don't half put a bit of spice back into our marriage.

Look at me, I'm fat, disabled and now I am fucking bald with stage four cancer and about a year to live if I'm lucky. The way I deal with it, is doing what the fuck I like.

'Well, I'm no prude dear, but you clearly have no morals to brag about it,' Audrey scoffed.

'Yes, I agree,' Sheila added in her way of supporting Audrey's comment.

'I just like cock,' Sue said with a shrug.

Debbie stood, 'Thank you ladies, I think it's time for an early tea break.'

'Thank Christ for that,' as Audrey sighed with relief.

The other six ladies sat and chatted among themselves, while Debbie prepared for the second session.

Sue was no longer centre of attention. The other ladies would never be able to look at her in the same light of day again and the dogging subject was never mentioned again within those four walls, however, Ronda belly laughed all the way home she found it most enlightening and it sure did take away some of her darkest days because each time things got her down, she thought about Sue and her shenanigans. It was better to cry real tears from the laughter, rather than sad tears over her prognosis.

Ronda, however, will always find it hard to believe that sort of thing actually goes on so close to home.

After refreshments Debbie opened the second half of the discussion group by suggesting alternative ways to feel good about their bodies. Once Debbie had complete control over the group, they ran thirty minutes over, and the ladies enjoyed sharing positive ideas that did not include dogging. Such as a spa day, Yoga, health and beauty, a good night's sleep but most importantly they each needed to love their own bodies again.

Not one of those ladies left without a dirty great grin on their face.

After running support groups and help lines as a volunteer for over ten long years, Ronda can honestly say she had never laughed so much in all her days and she would defiantly be joining the group again.

'Next time ladies the group will be discussing the impact of chemotherapy, focusing on chemo brain . . .'

# Chapter 21

## Results

Tick, tock, tick, tock - while Ronda anxiously waited for the dreaded phone call, she stared at the clock on the wall, watching the minute hand slowly move from one second to the next.

The heat wave over the last five days had been over bearing, as the sweat waterfalled down her neck into the small of her back. Her head pounded with intense pain, as her eyes itched her nose ran which was enough to tell the pollen count had hit another high that day.

The profound pain in her back had given her another restless night.

The clock had now moved by four minutes past the hour. The call was rarely ever on time. Tick, tock, tick, tock . . . Please dear God, let it be better news. Ronda had accepted it would never be good news, not now, not ever again, that ship had long sailed, but she prayed all the same.

All she ever heard was negative comments from her oncologist, while other people tell her to stay positive, what do they know? They know nothing, none of them do.

The previous scan results were good, the chemo had once again worked its magic and the cancer had shrunk, but not gone, maybe Ronda was expecting a miracle when she hoped it had gone altogether. That's what happens if we are over positive. It brings more disappointment. Think the worst then it can only be better.

Once again Ronda was on watch and wait. She was given three whole months of freedom to enjoy life before the next blood test.

'What a bloody relief to have all that treatment over and done with. I vow, I can never go through it ever again, I know, I know, I said that last time, knocked me for six, spoilt my Christmas, with that and bloody Covid adding to the mix, it turned my life upside down. I can hardly put into words how happy I'm feeling right now, on top of the flipping world. There's nothing like illness to make you appreciate everything you've got in life, and believe me I've got a lot. I might not have realized before but I do now. I don`t mind admitting there have been times when I have convinced myself I wasn't going to make it.'

After so much chemotherapy and other toxic drugs that made her feel poorly she came close to wishing she would close her eyes and never wake up. But that was all behind her now. The doctors were happy with the progress she was making and sent her a follow up appointment in six months.

After three months, Ronda's bloods had started to rise again but only by a very small amount which could have been down to anything. Her oncologist wasn't worried however, she decided to follow with another blood test within a six-week duration.

Again, her CA 125 marker test had risen ever so slightly, but not enough for concern. However, the blood tests showed a high elevation to her kidney function test and her liver was struggling enough to be a significant concern. Her bone density test came back with a low result too. How could there be so much change in as little as six weeks?

Ronda was fast tracked for another scan.

The waiting was terrifying - all Ronda could think about was the cancer had spread and she knew if her gut feeling was correct, she would be facing a huge fight to stay in this life for a while longer.

Ronda was aware there may be further treatment options but she wasn't daft, she knew this was getting closer to the end of life.

At three o'clock on a Thursday afternoon, Billy and Ronda sat in Café Nero in the beautiful historic market town of Stamford, when Billy's cell phone rang.

The noise from so much chatter echoed as it bounced off the walls making it difficult to hear. As Billy looked across the table for two into his wife's eyes, she knew the call was serious and her smile changed within an instant from happy to concern.

'Yes,' he said, 'I will pass the phone over,'

'Hello,' Ronda said in low voice.

'Hello Ronda, it`s Paula here from oncology. I have been instructed to organize a scan for you as soon as possible. Can you come next Wednesday or Friday?'

'Yes,' she replied, 'Wednesday would be good for me.'

'That`s great, it's an early appointment I`m afraid, we would like you in ACU - that's the Ambulatory Care Unit next to oncology, so you can park in car park F like when you come for chemo.'

'Okay.'

'It's a three-hour procedure before you have your scan and another three hours after your scan, this will potentially prevent you from developing further serious kidney problems associated with the scan. Does that make sense?'

'Yes, I think so.'

'I understand the oncologist has spoken to you last week and explained that your liver, kidney function is struggling, now this could be down to the hot weather and the fact you have been having a lot of severe hot sweating.'

'Yes, she mentioned that,' Ronda told her.

Ronda found all this quite daunting. She listened with great care to what the nurse was explaining - it sounded worse than it actually was, but it really left her quite shaken. I think it was the fact that she was out on a happy day, free from symptoms, a day she had forgotten about cancer, and all that doom and gloom that had over whelmed her far too many times over the past eleven years. Had it really been that long? The speed of time made her anxieties worse each time she thought about how much had actually happened during those years because of her health.

She finished her chai-latte and they walked back to the car. Neither of them was in the mood for anymore window shopping. It was time to go home.

For the first ten minutes of their journey back to Spalding neither of them spoke a word. Ronda was empty of thoughts; she just watched the sky line as Billy drove. Then he leaned over to take hold of her hand, and he looked at her with teary eyes and they both let it all out, they talked and cried and once Ronda had started there was no more holding back, she just cried and cried the rest of the way home.

By the time they were home Ronda was too tired to think about what they were going to eat for their evening meal. Billy sent her upstairs to rest; she was so exhausted she felt well poorly. She was like an old favourite teddy bear who had all his stuffing kicked out of him. She was limp and lifeless and before anyone could count to ten, she was sleeping on top of her duvet with the fan blowing over her over-heating body in order to cool her.

When she woke it was five thirty, she quickly freshened up and they made their way to the Tulip Queen for food. They had hit the happy hour and were unable to get a table. Instead, they picked up a kebab from the Indian across town.

It was hard to process the appointment Ronda had been offered for the following Wednesday, she had to be at the hospital by eight thirty in the morning. Although the government restrictions had been lifted for Covid 19, the hospital was still sticking to some of the rules so unfortunately Billy wouldn't be able to stay with her. He found that really quite difficult. Leaving his wife eight hours at the hospital just for another CT scan was out of the norm. This time Ronda had to face three hours of the intravenous drip of saline, to avoid any further damage to her kidneys, and another three hours after the scan to leave her well hydrated before she left the hospital. It was going to be a long day, a day no different to having chemo, Saline rather than the evil toxins of chemo, but still the same procedure and still a long day . . .

Ronda didn't know how to explain why she felt so anxious, it's just that it had always been straight forward before. She was pretty good at taking things in her stride but never-the-less it was another wakeup call, 'I have cancer, I have cancer,' she recited over and over inside her own head.

Lots of feelings with deep set emotions were backed in a queue, she knew if she broke, she wouldn't mend easily, now she had other health worries caused by the cancer treatments. She hadn't prepared herself for any of this. She wasn't going to make it, was she?

When Ronda's alarm woke her at an unearthly hour of six-thirty, she wondered what on earth was going on. No sooner than she remembered she wanted to throw the damn clock at the wall to smash it. Instead, she had to drag her tired feeble body across the room to wake herself up in a tepid shower.

It was on occasions like this she was glad of little hair to wash and certainly not enough to dry. She only bothered with makeup because she knew if she looked better, she would feel better and anything would be an improvement on looking and feeling this ill. So, she clogged her pores and carefully applied the lip gloss.

Her eye lashes were still sparse, so she only applied eye liner, and she had had her eye brows tattooed, so no worries there. She gave herself some slack from the wig, it was going to be another sweltering day and it can be anything from baking hot or freezing cold from the air conditioning. Besides the wigs were itchy and she didn`t need to inflict any more discomfort on herself.

'Do not arrive any earlier than five minutes before your appointment time,' the letter from the hospital stated.

'Please wear a face covering before entering the hospital, this can be a mask, a scarf or something else.

Please use the hand sanitizer that is provided for our patients as you enter the building.

'Please attend your appointment alone. Unfortunately, a friend or relative is not allowed to accompany you on this occasion, due to the Covid 19 virus.'

'I guess that counts Billy out then,' Ronda huffed. She wondered if she lied and said she got severe panic attacks, would they let him stay with her? But it wouldn't be on her notes. Besides she needed to be a little bit independent, otherwise she would soon be joining the crack head section.

'I will be bloody pleased when this Covid palaver has done one, I`ve bloody had enough.' She muttered to any bugger in hearing distance!

They arrive at the hospital at twenty minutes past the hour.

'It`s okay,' Ronda told her husband.

'You can go, I`ll be alright - unless . . .' She paused,

'You want me to ask if you can stay.'

'I was wondering that,' he said, 'but we`ve left the cats in.'

'Oh yer, I forgot about our fur babies.'

Pause . . .

'Well, we don`t want to get home and find anything unpleasant stuck to the carpets.' Ronda told her husband.

'I will come in with you though, make sure you check in okay, if they allow me too.'

Billy opened the car boot and reached for her bag, 'Got all you need?' he asked kindly.

'Enough to keep me occupied for eight bloody hours,' she chortled.

They waited for the electric doors to open and report their arrival at the reception desk.

'Hello, I am Ronda Stone, I have an appointment for eight thirty,' she said.

The chubby blonde receptionist, looked at the screen in front of her . . .

'What name is it again?' she asked.

'Ronda Stone,'

'What are you booked in for?' she asked in a kind voice.

'IV hydration for three hours before and after my scan.'

'I don`t seem to have you listed, do you have an appointment letter?' confused as she asked with her eye brows raised to the heavens.

Before handing over her letter, Ronda checked the date. 'It is the eleventh today isn`t it?'

'NO, you numpty,' Billy chuckled, 'that's next Wednesday.'

'But the nurse who phone definitely said next week, and that was last week, making next week this week. Oh, never mind, see you next week then,' she told the receptionist with a giggle.

The three of them laughed in unison, and Billy and Ronda walked back to the car.

You really couldn't make it up, could you? All that tummy churning nonsense with nerves and running to the loo in urgency every five minutes, after all that she had the wrong flipping week.

'Never mind.' she told Billy, 'Hey, we can go for a McDonalds breakfast, I am never out and about early enough, but today we are,' she said like an excited 7 year-old.

'If that's what you want darling, then that's what you shall have,'

'Thanks,' she said snuggling up to him before they drove off.

'So, what are we going to do for the rest of the day?' Ronda wanted to know while she sipped her latte.

It was home first to let the cats out. Then after a couple of phone calls, they decided to meet Bella and family in Norfolk.

It was fun to watch the grandchildren in the Sandringham estate's play area, set up by the lovely Catherine Windsor.

Then they all met up again on Heacham Beach, Billy

and Ronda stayed for a couple of hours then headed back to Spalding for a Sheddies, Fish and Chip tea.

The others stayed on the beach until eight in the evening, the kiddies mudded up to the eye balls. They managed to have a nice fish and chip tea from Heacham.

What a lovely day that turned out to be, in the end.

'We have to make the most of the nice weather,' Billy said.

'Indeed, we do, and making memories,' Ronda added with a yawn.

*Days like that are so precious . . .*

'I expect you're tired little darling, aren't you?' Billy said lovingly.

'Yes, but in a good way.'

'Let's get you off to bed.'

Ronda's eyes immediately lit up with a sparkle, 'No Ronda,' Billy grinned, 'you need your rest,'

'I know I do, but I need you more.'

# Chapter 22

## Wednesday August 11<sup>th</sup>, 2021.

Buzz, Buzz, Buzz hummed the alarm clock at six thirty sharp. Billy and Ronda had a deja vu journey as the week before, the traffic was busy, while everyone drove to work carefully.

'Let's hope there's no cock-ups this week,' Billy chortled with some indignation.

'I'd much sooner be having that McDonalds' breakfast again,' Ronda chuckled.

'If you are a good girl I will order one to be delivered tomorrow,' Billy, sounded as though he was talking to one of their grandchildren. But Ronda didn't mind one bit, she felt like a child on days like this, scared and shaky, it never seemed to get any easier.

'Small sharp scratch,' they always warn as they are about to stab you with the needle.

'I don't know why, you nurses always say that,' Ronda said, 'It feels nothing like a scratch.'

'Sorry,' nurse Lucy apologized.

'No worries,' Ronda told her, 'I never felt a thing. I always say you can tell a good nurse, by the needle Christ-all-ruddy-mighty, some of them are not as gentle, I often think, if her over there can do it without me feeling anything, then why can`t you,'

Lucy laughed, 'That's a good point.'

Once the cannula was secure in a good vein the intravenous drip was rigged up, that's all there was to it for the next three hours.

She was in a small room, but at least it had a window, a few minutes passed and another patient came to take the second chair. It was different to the chemo ward, with two to six chairs set out along each wall.

Here, there were several small rooms, two patients to a room, but it was a mixed ward like the chemo and many others these days, let's just say it's something you get used to. Anyway, Ronda didn`t mind at all, sometimes she felt more comfortable talking to a stranger than she did her own family, even if they were male.

On this occasion she shared the room with a fifty-two-year-old chap from Essex.

Ronda had gone armed with her note pad, pen and pencil to write to a friend who prefered to exchange letters the old-fashioned way. Ronda met Rachel on holiday in Turkey, which is quite a story to tell really. They always say you meet new people for a very good reason. At the end of their holiday the two women exchanged addresses, it was uncanny that Rachel lived in the next county to Ronda. Although, Lincolnshire is the largest county in the UK, Ronda lived right on the edge to Cambridgeshire, less than an hour away. When Ronda discovered her new friend only lived in Wisbech, she was delighted, but on her return home she couldn`t find Rachels address, and when Rachel failed to get in touch, Ronda felt a little sad.

The following year, Ronda and her family went back to Turkey and stayed in the exact same hotel as they had done the previous year. For some unknown reason they were not meant to keep in touch throughout the year. It was uncanny how the two couples holidays crossed over.

Billy left Ronda unpacking, while he went to say hello to some of the bar staff.

'You never guess who I have just bumped into in reception.'

'No, who?'

You remember that couple who had a daughter the same age as our Bella?'

'No, there were after all several,' she told her husband.

'The stuck-up bitch, who thought she was better than anyone else her age.'

'Oh, I think I know the one, her father got stung with a huge bill for the laundry of their towels because the daughter got make-up all over them.'

'I don`t know darling, but they are here again and their room is directly above ours.'

'Oh wow, what a small world, hopefully the daughter will be a little more friendly this year.'

'I doubt our Bella will give a Jack shit, she will be too interested in Tom and Gerry and the rest of the animation team, if they are here again this year. And guess who else is here too?'

'Just spit it out, and hang your shirts on the hangers, will you,'

'Okay, snappy knickers,' pause . . .

'Who then?'

'That couple from Wisbech.'

'Really.'

'Only prob darling, they are front of reception, all packed up and waiting for the bus to take them to the airport.'

'Oh no, you're kidding, are you telling me they have finished their holiday as ours begins.'

'Yep, sorry babes.'

By the time Ronda had run to reception, she caught a glimpse of the coach driving out of the Hotel's forecourt.

She shrugged it off as though it was not meant to be but while she continued to unpack, lo and behold she found Rachel's address tightly tucked under some tissue paper in one of the side pockets.

The first thing Ronda did when she got back was send Rachel a long newsy letter, and now they have been writing by hand and sending through royal mail for over almost two decades. She quite often killed the time on her chemo days to write to her friend. So, today that was what she intended to do.

The only problem was the very nice chap she shared her room with that day talked too much.

To be fair, they got along so well that day it was really nice to meet him.

The hours ticked fast and before she knew it the first three hours were up and it was time for the porter to take her down for the scan. She was gone a good hour and then she had at least another three hours on the intravenous drip before home.

The afternoon didn't seem to pass so quickly, by the time she was let out, she gulped the air as though she had been locked away for decades. It must have been one of the nicest summer days they'd had and she was stuck inside on a flipping drip, just because she hadn't been looking after herself very well, and that's what she had to tell herself. If the hydration treatment didn`t work for her, it could only mean one of two evils, either the cancer had spread or she needed to be referred to a kidney specialist. There was no mention about her bone density or poor liver function, but no doubt that would all be discussed at the next oncology appointment. In the meantime, all she could do was pray for her life and keep making love to her wonderful husband.

Ronda always said, 'No news, is good news,' but after waiting two weeks, Billy's anxiety was starting to irritate Ronda beyond what her patience would allow.

'So, you ring the nurse and ask, if you are so worried,' knowing full well the results wouldn`t be in yet. Ronda thought it best if he found out for himself because whatever she said didn`t seem to put his mind at ease.

However, his phone call wasn`t totally wasted, he did manage to find out that there had been no change with her kidney function test. Which was a bit of a shock, because they had all hoped the hydration would have helped with the problem, so now they had no idea why her kidney function was below an acceptable level. Her liver and bones density were not re-tested, so it was still possible the cancer had now progressed into these other organs.

In the meantime, Ronda developed excruciating pain in her urethra making peeing painful and difficult, and she was now starting to pass blood. She had had this before; most women are familiar to the symptoms of cystitis and Ronda certainly did seem to have an increase in her libido. They don`t call it the honeymoon disease for nothing. What did seem to alarm her was she had had these same symptoms at the time she was diagnosed with her cancer re-occurrence, one chemo later had shrunk the tumour enough to ease it away from her bladder. It was possible this was caused by tumour progression and nothing more. In which case, Ronda had to tell herself another round of chemo would do the trick. But, how much longer can she keep going through this before the chemo fails her?

For now, another appointment had been made in the beginning of September to talk with her oncologist, in the meantime, they would be chasing up the scan results.


One thing Ronda couldn`t be doing with was Billy`s mithering – he`d become a right old nag. While he needed to absorb her strength, she felt drained by his anxieties.

'Stay positive,' they say. Then when we do, we are floored by the next blow, it is like a roller coaster of events. It`s good to be positive but, if we are not, we are judged about being in denial. We also do need to face up to the reality of disease progression. At the end of the day, it is what it is and no matter how strong we appear to be on the outside deep down we are falling apart. Besides we can`t be brave all of the time.


She told her doctor she was depressed, 'I am not treating you for depression,' he told her 'It`s perfectly normal to feel the way you do, considering what you are going through.'

Friday evening on August 28th 2021, the landline buzzed at precisely seven-twenty, just as Emmerdale was reaching its peak of interest. Billy reached for the phone . . .

'Yes,' he said with a frown, 'I will just pass you over.'

The look on her husband's face and the tone in his voice was enough to tell Ronda it was serious.

'Hello Ronda, it's Paula from the hospital.'

'Oh, hello,' Ronda said surprised to hear from the hospital on a Friday evening.

'Now, I don't want you to worry too much, but I understand you have an appointment to see Dr Ayers next Thursday afternoon.' Ronda confirmed that was correct, while Paula continued to ask her an awful lot of questions.

'I am a bit concerned about the blood test results from Monday. Although there is still no change since the hydration, I wondered how you are feeling in yourself as I understand from Kelly you have been quite poorly this week.' The questions that followed were all in line with the cystitis symptoms.

'Kelly is not in over the weekend and I can't get hold of Dr Ayers so the decision is left to me. I have your scan results in front of me and it seems that your tumour is putting an awful lot of strain on your kidney's, so I need to have a word with the renal team and the on-call oncologist, I will call you back soon,'

When the phone buzzed again, Ronda picked up. 'Hello again, it's Paula, an appointment has been made tomorrow morning at eleven o'clock, at the ambulatory unit, next to the oncology unit. Unfortunately, you will be asked to wait an hour and a half for the results. Then we will be able to decide what the next step will be.'

'Okay,' Ronda agreed.

'I will need you to bring an overnight bag with you as we may need to keep you in overnight to have a stent put in, which will make you more comfortable before you see Dr Ayers on Thursday.

'Dare I ask about the scan results?' Ronda asked.

'A MDT meeting will take place on Tuesday afternoon and your case will be discussed then. By Thursday afternoon Sarah will be able to explain what the next treatment plan will be for you.

This was nothing less than she expected, the old grim was progressing at an alarming rate and now they were talking about palliative intent.

Suddenly, Ronda felt floored as the tears started to sting as she welled up. But she held it together and did not cry as her mother's words rang clear – 'No tears sweetheart, be a brave soldier, remember you have got this.'

*A strong person is not the one who doesn`t cry.*
*A strong person is one who is quiet and shed tears for a moment,*
*And picks up the sword and fights again . . .*

By the time the phone calls between Paula and Ronda had finished it was eight-forty-five. She had missed the best part of Emmerdale and the first half of Coronation Street. She smiled, as she remembered watching it with her mother in the sixties, when Hilda Ogden wore curlers under her blue headscarf that matched her blue paisley apron, fag in gob while she sang out in the highest decibels as she pegged out Stan's string vests in the yard.

For now, Ronda needed to focus on packing a hospital bag. She decided if she packed for a week, it would never happen and she would be able to come home to sleep that night.

She did not wish for a daja vu experience of eleven years ago. She pinched herself to remind her this would be a breeze in comparison, and nothing as invasive as her bilateral breast surgery. This however, did not mean she found sleep easily, she felt so totally trolleyed but sleep wouldn`t come or at least not until she had finished the conversation with herself.

She woke again at seven thirty the next morning. She stayed relaxed until closer to eight when she switched on the shower and 'wagons rolled.' Billy was already in the kitchen making a pot of breakfast tea.

Ten minutes before they were ready to leave for the hospital – 'ping,' went her tablet.

Shit! Shit! Shit! She had totally forgotten about winning the bid for the Ted Baker handbag in a matter of minutes before Paula's call the previous evening. Ronda had already arranged with the seller to pay and collect from Sleaford on the Saturday afternoon.

Even if she was released from the hospital in time, it was a fifty-six-mile trip from Peterborough City Hospital. The only thing Ronda could do was message the seller and explain the situation.

As expected, only patients were allowed in the clinic. Although the government had lifted the covid restrictions, the hospital Ronda was to attend that day had reversed back to safety measures as the Covid cases had increased. Poor Billy was left waiting in the car. It was a lovely sunny day but by no means too hot to bear, which was a small blessing.

Ronda's blood test appointment was delayed by twenty minutes which wasn`t a great start. By the time her name was called and her bloods had been taken it was eleven forty-five by the time she was back in the car park pulling Billy up to speed. Now they had the long wait of one hour and thirty minutes before Ronda would know if she was going to be admitted or not.

Billy managed to get a machine coffee from the main atrium when he discovered costa coffee didn`t open over the weekends. So much for killing some time. Luckily, he had taken a banana and apple to keep him going. Ronda was offered a hot drink and biscuits from the nurse who had taken her bloods. This was greatly appreciated, alongside the book she had taken to read, and the hour and thirty minutes soon passed.

Paula wasn`t on weekend duty however, she had asked a colleague to keep an eye out for Ronda.

On arrival, as Paula had suggested, Ronda called the emergency number to let Sabia know she had arrived. Sabia was also a nurse specialist and she had come down to greet Ronda with another nurse who called her through for her consultation. Both nurses were wonderful and they always seemed to go out of their way to make Ronda feel special.

Ronda was delighted to be told that her kidney function had increased ever so slightly and because Ronda looked and felt so well, they were happy to send her home . . . by two o/clock Billy was driving them back to Spalding for a much-needed cup of tea and bite to eat, followed by a twenty-five mile drive to Sleaford to collect the bag.

TED BAKER Bag here we come!

Ronda had never been to Sleaford market town before – so close to home and yet so far . . . The one-way system took them through the town centre. She was pleasantly surprised by the amount of restaurants and outside drinking zones, all secluded under cover cubes with surrounding fake hedging and undercover. It was definitely a place to visit again before the summer's end. On a nice day you could imagine yourself anywhere on the continent. Even the charity shops looked inviting, a massive improvement on Spalding's town centre.

They found the address easily enough along the Boston Road or at least the sat-nav took them to where they needed to be. Parking was impossible, with either single or double yellow lines going on forever. The distance to the end terrace of Victorian town houses to the first available parking was too far for Ronda to manage, so Billy parked on a double yellow with Ronda's disability parking badge on display, he waited in the car. She was only gone five minutes, so even that little adventure turned out to be more positive.

The neat row of houses looked grubby and unkempt from years of dirt and grime from the busy main road. Ronda`s belly was doing a U turn, what was she thinking of, buying a second-hand bag from somewhere so off putting.

By the time she had reached number ninety-five, Ronda was relieved to find that one house stood out from the rest. The windows and door were clean from the weather battering the others had endured. Expensive looking curtains and blinds hung inside the windows, with fresh cut flowers in a vase. A pretty summer wreath hung on the door above the highly polished door knocker.

This was more than a house; it was a home, proudly owned with lots of love.

A young immaculately dressed mum answered the door, with a toddler straddled around her hip. A big wide smile to welcome her.

It turned out the run-off-her-feet single mum of two had her own hairdressing business in town, like Ronda in her younger years.

'It's a small world, isn`t it?' Ronda told her. 'Both of my daughters are hairdressers too,'

The two women chatted a little about how busy the hairdressing trade has been since the end of lock down. It was so nice to know that such businesses have pulled through the never-ending pandemic.

Ronda was very pleased with her purchases and said her good buys with a nice smile to greet Billy back at the car.

Before home they called in to see Bella and the grandchildren. Lizzies' daughter Molly was staying for a sleep over with Ellenor. The two little girls sat happily on the sofa, playing a game on their tablets, while little Jake played happily by himself on the floor.

'My goodness, I have never known the house so quiet,' Ronda told them.

'Look Grandma,' Jake implored before she had time to kick her shoes off. 'Look Grandma, look,' he squealed in excitement.

'Oh, lovely, what have you got there?' Granny Ronda wanted to know.

'COWS, Grandma and I have PIGS too,' after a short pause he offered her a funny looking duck with a long yellow beak that had a pouch under its chin, 'What is it?' Jake asked.

Once the excitement in the room had waned Ronda gave her grandson an in-depth explanation about the difference between a DUCK and a PELICAN.

'What's his pouch for?' Jake wanted to know.

'Well, a pelican eats a lot of fish, and as he scoops the fish up with his long beak, it drops into his pouch, so he can carry it away to eat. It's a bit like mummy`s shopping basket.'

'Where we put things, when we shop on line? Or at the supermarket?' he added

'Exactly like that,' Grandma told him.

'Wow, you know everything Grandma,' he told her with a big grin that beamed from ear to ear, while Ellenor and Molly sniggered behind their hand.

As it turned out Molly didn`t stay to sleep. Uncle Chris took her home at ten o'clock that evening. He could tell by the look on her face that she really wanted to stay but also really, really didn`t.

'I think if mummy is really, really cross I might change my mind and stay after all,' she told her uncle.

They do make us smile, even if they do rule the roost these days.

As for Ronda, she was so exhausted after her own day, she was actually in bed sleeping long before the grandchildren.

*Grandchildren help us to find the important things we may have lost . . .*
*Your smile, your hope, and your courage!*
*They help us stay strong until things get better, after all the rain doesn`t last forever . . .!*

# Chapter 23

## 'Chocolate Cheesecake'

It was mid-summer on a Friday afternoon, the sun shone down upon them as they glided through the small market town of Holbeach in Lincolnshire, Ronda's birth place.

She was having a better day today, it was nice to escape from the four walls of their luxurious home to bake in the sun. It was a lot easier now the government had lifted the tight covid restrictions of the pandemic. There were still a few nervous people out there, especially the few who had still not been vaccinated, mostly by their own choice. There would always be a few who chose to wear a face covering, although most were sick to the back teeth of them.

Ronda gained her confidence by slowly returning back to normal, registered as highly vulnerable while she was having cancer treatment gave her little choice but to strictly self-isolate, when many people ignored the advice given by the government.

She observed the dog walkers along the river bank stopping to chat with one another, with no mask and no safe distance between them. A few of these were her next-door neighbours. The news made her paranoid as it did many others. She was now fighting two dilemmas: Cancer and Covid. She did not feel safe until after their second vaccination. She yearned to hug her grandchildren; she began to feel she may never do so again. Watching the news to see over crowded beaches during the summer 2020 was madness. Then there were the riots in London, 'Black Lives Matter!' Of course, they do, but they were missing the point by putting every other individual's life at risk while expressing themselves. People were being labelled as racist when they really, really weren't. I mean, for goodness' sake they chose their time to shout out loud, didn`t they just?

So Ronda chose to hibernate while she no longer listened to the news.

Ronda's cancer was showing signs of progression again, but for now she was not having treatment and she was as safe as anyone else could be. She had her own personal reasons for not wearing a face mask, although she did in the busy shops and hospitals. A lot of places she simply avoided altogether. In other words, she was probably one of the safest people walking along the High Street. However, when she chose it wasn't necessary to wear a face covering she did not expect anyone to hector her into it especially when logic made no sense, maybe that made her arrogant, although she was blinded by that suggestion and would most probably bite anyone's head off who suggested as such. Truth be told her complexion was suffering with red itchy blotches and even worse, acne, from wearing the ruddy things. She had never even had acne in her teens, the odd spot maybe, but at sixty-three this felt tragic. Besides who thought about her wishes when she was clinically vulnerable? Did she run around insisting all and sundry should wear a face mask? Of course not, so she didn`t appreciate anyone telling her to now.

They enjoyed a stroll along the High Street heading for a delightful little tea room which offered a wonderful selection of light bites, homemade cakes, puddings and every label of tea and coffee you could think of. It was a little more expensive than the normal place but it seemed to be the only little tea shop in plain sight.

The few tables and chairs that were set out on the public pavement were already taken, but they didn't seem to be spaced out enough, which made Ronda uneasy. Besides, who wants to sit along a dusty busy road with so much traffic noise? So Billy and Ronda went inside . . . hand sanitizing before they went in. There were only a couple of ladies having afternoon tea, two steps down into the tiny snug area on the right side of the entrance. There was half a wall dividing them from the main seating area, making them well secluded from the counter. The rest of the tables were unoccupied. Ronda literally had two steps in the door when she placed her bag on the table for two in the bay window, turning on the same spot to check out the wonderful display of cakes.

The small business was owned by a couple of queers, as bent as a nine-bob bit, her mother would have scoffed, but heaven help anyone who said such a thing today. The campest of the pair answered to the name of Justin, he was clean shaven and very handsome, Ronda envied his clear complexion. He smelt divine; he wore gold diamond stud earrings in each ear; an immaculately pressed pink paisley shirt, neatly tucked into the front of his navy-blue denim jeggings and left to flow freely out of the waist band to overhang his tiny buttocks. He wore a plain navy silk bow tie under his collar. His large pink topaz ring worn on his middle finger, right hand, caught the light above making it glisten and sparkle, picking up the colours in the décor. He wore a wide white gold wedding band on his third finger left hand. Tan leather lace up shoes that shone to a mirror finish caught your eye immediately. The shoes on their own would have cost hundreds. He simply oozed good taste and wealth.

He wasn`t wearing a face mask but he chose to wear a visor. Displaying his prefect white veneered smile. His was a natural medium blonde with a few bleached highlights, cut into a neat short back and sides that had clearly been freshly styled that morning.

The first words he spoke from the other side of the screen that divided them at the counter were, 'Good afternoon, how can I help you?'

'Two lattes please, and . . .' before Ronda could say chocolate cheesecake, he blurted, 'You need to hand sanitize,'

'We have,' she answered correctly.

'Well, you need to be wearing a face covering while you stand, to order at the counter.'

'Do you offer table service?' Ronda asked.

'Yes, but first you need to wear a face covering, have you got one with you?'

Ronda rummaged through her bag, while Billy said he would run back to the car to fetch his.

He went on to tell them, once they were seated, they could remove the mask and order.

Ronda turned and sat on the seat where she had left her bag, smiled sweetly and said, 'There, problem solved, I am sat, so can I please include a chocolate cheese cake with my order? Thank you.' Ronda`s mother always told her sarcasm was the lowest form of wit, but it didn't stop her acid tongue.

'I will take your order once you are wearing a face mask,' he chided.

'Once I'm seated, you mean?'

'No, while you stand at the counter and order your food,' he told her abruptly.

Ronda's mother also used to say 'It's not always what you say that makes an impact, it's the way you say it,' and it was the way he said it, that got right up her nose.

'Yes, I understand that, but you tell us after we have walked through the door and told you what we would like to order.'

'Yes, but you still have to wear a face mask,' he insisted.

This was beginning to get really childish now, 'and take it off when I sit down?'

'Yes.'

'So, I am sat down now and taken my face mask off.'

'Yes, but you need to put it back on when you walk over to the counter to place your order.'

'Well, it's a little late now, this is a bit like closing the gate after the horse has bolted, you have already taken our order.'

'And I am asking you to now wear a face covering, because you need to pay at the counter.'

'You could always sit outside,' Mr Loved-Himself, suggested.

'No, we couldn't, we'll just leave then, shall we?' and she stood and squeezed past him to get out of the door as quickly as possible, leaving Ronda as wound up as a coiled spring, and rant did she – all the way back to the car!

'What a twat,' Ronda scoffed.

'No, he certainly hasn`t got one of those,' Billy chuckled, finding Ronda extremely funny.

'Well, he thinks he has, when really he`s just a wanker,' she spat.

'Ronda . . .' Billy laughed loudly.

'WHAT,' she hissed.

'You never swear, anyone would think you had just had a day on the building site,'

'What building site.'

'Never mind darling,' he said putting his arms around her to give her a great big bear hug.

'Well, it's enough to make a saint swear,' she told him, 'He can stuff his fucking cheesecake where the sun don`t shine,'

'Yes, darling,' Billy agreed, he knew right or wrong it was never a good time to argue, once Ronda was on a roll.

Once Ronda had calmed down, she knew she was being disrespectful, but to her it had no logic.

Besides where is this 'customer is always right shit?' that was always drummed into her brain when she was training in customer care. It never seemed to apply when the boot was on the other foot. Silly sod, and now instead of recommending the place to all her friends, she told everyone the story . . . and Ronda and Billy would never step foot anywhere near the place again.

As she dozed off in her husband's arms, she had a

thought . . . 'Billy, are you asleep yet?'

'I was,' he told her.

'I just thought . . .'

'Hmm.'

'If we could have sat outside to solve the no mask situation.'

'Yer.'

'How could we have paid at the counter?'

Billy burst in to laughter, 'I expect we would have paid at the table outside'

'So, why couldn`t we have paid from the table inside?' she wanted to know!

'Because we were inside, not outside.'

'I don`t understand the difference,' she mused.

'Go to sleep,' he told her after tenderly kissing her forehead.

'Night, night.'

'Night, night, love you.'

'Love you too.'

# Chapter 24

## 'One day at a time'

Ronda felt herself floating along one day at a time, leaving all the angst and strife of her insignificant little life behind.

She was in a tea shop on a Tuesday afternoon, counselling a friend who had more woes than Ronda could possibly have had right now. Her friend didn't mention the 'C' word, she never did, she couldn't bare it - or didn't know how. She should spend a little more time to listen rather than talk, talk, talk so much.

She was like a vampire sucking her blood dry. The exhaustion showed as dark circles appeared under her eyes. She tried to switch her off for a second while she reached into her bag to find a nice bright shade of pink lippy. She looked into the small leather Radley mirror that went everywhere with her, not that she was vain or anything, but she did like her lippy, with every good intention to help her feel better, even if it didn`t.

She noticed her own complexion had changed from rosy to a pale shade of grey, and yet her friend didn't notice and continued to yap, yap, yap about her bloody self or people Ronda didn't know, with the odd jibe, that felt as though it was targeted at her. She made no comment, she just sat and pretended to listen.

Feeling the pulse thumping in her head, her neck and shoulders felt heavier by the minute.

She screamed inside her own mind with satanic

thoughts that began to overwhelm her.

She wanted to tell her involving sexual promiscuity and drugs was going about it the wrong way.

She wants to say, 'I`m not interested in other people's shenanigans - stop, stop, stop.' She seethed in her own private bubble. 'I've heard it a million times before.'

As her friend sat in her psychedelic dress with her, to-die-for figure, Ronda looked at her wondering how she`d ever cope if cancer was happening to her right now? Would she want to talk about it then?

Ronda was so, so tired, that bloody cockerel started crowing at four am, 'Cock-a-doodle-errrrr!'

She knew the cock was Bristolian because of the 'errrrr.' She wished the thing would do one and skedaddle right back to where it came from, instead of loitering around her neighbourhood.

The town Centre was as depressed as she felt, so many more shops had closed after the pandemic, it was such a shame. Hills department store had been taken over by Coney`s. Still a fabulous shop and apart from the new wine bar in the midst of the cooking area, nothing much had changed. However, the store was empty apart from a minimum of six sitting on the high bar stools. Ronda noticed a nice quirky outside area, but the day was too grey to sit outside. August had been a grim month in more ways than one.

As Covid restrictions waned, the weather had an Autumn damp chill in the air. It was too humid to wear a thin jacket but there was no sun, Ronda complained how clammy the atmosphere was. A good storm may have cleared the air but the forecast did not offer rain, not today anyway. The town centre had a dead atmosphere, with nothing more to offer than two expensive shops, one decent shoe shop, a couple of pharmacies, loads of charity shops and coffee shops all of which have gone downhill, and no one seems to be doing any business apart from M & Co, Greggs and all the hairdressing salons. As Ronda turned over the stale Victoria sponge and sipped on the strong latte, she felt an overwhelming sadness as she reminisced how Spalding used to be back in the day. What would her dear Mum think to it now? Nothing stays the same, but usually things should change for the better. There was nothing better about the town on this day. Even all the good public houses were boarded up. So, many jobs lost. Where can all those people work now?

Ronda went to the counter to pay the bill – how could such a dreadful offering have cost over twelve pounds. Everywhere was expensive these days and have you noticed the price of afternoon tea? A maximum of two slices of bread and even then, they go cutting the crusts off, such a waste her mother would say. When you stop to think how our parents encouraged us to eat the crust - as if they really would make our hair curl. Who wanted curly hair in any case? And now everyone cut the bloody crusts off to make them look neater on the plate, for goodness' sake. Ronda decided, the next time she ordered a sandwich she would insist she got her money`s worth and they could bloody well leave the crust intact. Oh, she did feel in a tetchy mood today, in fact she couldn`t wait to get home to a proper latte and a slice of homemade cake, freshly baked yesterday.

Ronda continued in her own thoughts as she waited for someone to take her dosh, 'Hello, is anyone there?' she called in a sarcastic tone. It wasn`t as though they were busy or short staffed, she could hear laughter coming from the kitchen. Honestly, Ronda and her friend were the only customers and they couldn`t even bother to take their payment.

The lady came rushing through the swing doors behind the counter, not as though she had anyone else to rush for. 'Sorry about that,' she said, 'I was just …….' she couldn`t finish her sentence because truth be told she was just chatting with her mates in the kitchen about the previous night's drama.

'That's Okay,' Ronda chuckled, 'I have all day.'

Her friend walked out of the shop to wait outside - too embarrassed to stay. There were a few pretty items in the shop, Ronda would have purchased but she wasn`t in the mood to offer them anymore custom, so she floated out of the door into the fresh air.

'Where to now then Mrs.?' her friend wanted to know. But Ronda was so dreadfully drained from hearing all the drama in her friend's pathetic excuse of a life, all she had the strength to do now was go home to bed.

They walked together to the car park where they had met earlier and parted their ways. Ronda, dragged her tired body to her car. She lifted her heavy legs into the foot well and started her up. She lifted the gears into reverse and took off the hand brake, then she decided on impulse to go back into town alone, and treat herself to a jacket she had spotted in M & Co. It was hopeless trying to concentrate on shopping while her mate continued to drone on about, 'he said, she said, I said!'

She was getting so wound up, Ronda wanted to scream 'Shut the fuck up,' Usually Ronda is pretty good at switching off, or at least she had mastered the act when Billy munched on his spittle. Something about this friend made her want to listen. One thing about the aftermath of chemotherapy, you lose the art of multi-tasking and Ronda was finding it ever more difficult to listen to any one ear aching in her lug holes, while she was trying to do something else.

Anyway, now you know!

As Ronda walked away from her locked car, it slowly started to reverse towards the line of cars a couple of rows behind. OMG, she panicked and ran to the driver's door. Of course, it was locked and the car was moving slightly faster down a very slight incline one would never even notice. Her keys had dropped into the bottom of her bag, the more she rushed the more she started to shake. She clicked the fob and managed to grab the door handle, but she wasn`t strong enough to halt the car from running away with itself, neither were her arms long enough to reach for the hand brake. Her legs were being pulled under the moving vehicle – she managed to pull the hand brake up seconds before her front wheel ran over her legs!

The car came to a lucky halt within an inch of the stationary car`s bumper. Ronda collapsed in a heap on the concrete and started to cry. A cat having five lives came into mind.

She was shaking so much; she was in no fit state to drive home yet. 'What the hell,' she told herself, 'I think this deserves more than a new jacket,' and off she went shopping.

Ronda could not explain why she should be surprised or disappointed in some of her so-called friends. After all, it wasn't as though they had't let her down before.

The support, love and care hadn't always come from the ones she had known the longest or those Ronda had offered hour upon hour of counselling in their time of need.

Even family ran a mile when you needed them the most, or continued to ask favours off you. They soon paid a visit when they wanted to vent about their own trivial nonsense though.

The ones Ronda would describe as one-sided friends had simply done one! Not a word, phone call, card, nada! Why? It wasn't as though cancer is contagious, and sure lock-down had't been easy for anyone, but all the more reason to pick up the phone or post a card, with just a few simple words inside. They did not even Face book message her, did she not matter?

The ones who had always left it to Ronda to make contact, continued to do so. Well, it wasn't happening any more. And if they were wondering how odd it was for Ronda to forget their birthday or Christmas, then they should contact her to see how she was doing. But they didn't, those sorts never did, if you failed to remember their birthday, then they conveniently remembered to forget yours. But they never thanked you, when you did remember.

Ronda understood others were not like her, some were just rubbish with words so they felt silence was the best option, but for God's sake was it rocket science? Ronda's mother always said, 'If you can`t say something kind, then best you say naught at all.'

'She had heard a barrow load of words that should be unsaid . . . Some had the nerve to tell her how lucky she was. Yup, Ronda, LUCKY! Some folks have some brain cells missing.

When someone you know is fighting a deadly illness like cancer, they do not want to hear all about your old age problems, they may have those too but just don`t mention it to you. Instead, they accept it because that's what they do best and they have little choice to only take one step at a time.

It's actually really nice when people tell you how well you look, only you know it's because you do everything in your power to do so, but even that can be insulting if they mean you can`t possibly be seriously ill, they are wrong.

While some continue to go about their daily business with decorum, someone will be feeling like crap, their life can be falling apart but to look at them you would never know. The truth is those who fall apart in their own personal state of mind, may cry with silent tears, they may feel unloved by some, forgotten by others.

You find out who matters and who shouldn`t, Ronda had one friend who took her wherever she wanted to go.

Another chatted every day and they got together whenever they could.

Others stayed in touch with comforting words.

Another friend wrote long letters and posted them

snail mail, others send an email.

*Everyone wants happiness, nobody wants pain,*
*But you can`t have a rainbow without a little rain.*

*I truly appreciate kindness, I appreciate people*
*checking up on me,*
*I appreciate those who ask if I`m okay.*
*I appreciate every single person in my life who has*
*tried to brighten my day.*
*It`s the little things that often matter the most,*

*Life is too short to wake in the morning with regrets,*
*So, love the people who treat you right and forget all*
*the rest.*
*Believe that everything happens for a reason . . .*
*If you get a chance then take it, if it changes your life*
*then let it,*
*Nobody said it would be easy . . .*
*They just promised it would be worth it.*

*Don`t wait for things to get easier, simpler or better,*
*Life will always be complicated,*
*Learn to be happy right now,*
*Otherwise, you will run out of time.*

*A huge shoutout to, the people who haven`t felt Okay*
*lately,*
*but still get up every day and refuse to quit,*
*remember whoever you are, you have got this . . .*

Quotes from; Love my Snoopy, Power of Positivity
and The Best of Health.

# Chapter 25

## Thursday 2ⁿᵈ September

It seemed to be a long harrowing day, Ronda's oncologist appointment wasn`t until three o'clock in the afternoon.

The morning dragged as Ronda and her husband prepared themselves for what they had already figured out for themselves.

Just as they had expected, the disease had progressed at an aggressive rate and in as little as six weeks Ronda's cancer was now causing a great deal of discomfort. Her kidney function test had fallen from a healthy sixty to twenty-seven, serious right?

The cancer had wrapped itself around the ureter, the tube from the walnut sized organ to the bladder causing excruciating pain when she tried to pee.

She spent a whole day unable to urinate, the fact that she had drunk three pints of water had made little difference. She just dribbled in agonizing pain for twenty-four hours, and then a little blood.

A decision had been made at the MDT meeting, that Ronda would most certainly benefit from a stent, even maybe two stents, the decision would be made on the day. Her oncologist explained that she would receive an appointment in the post for the procedure to take place sometime over the following two weeks. Ronda will be awake throughout the operation, but heavily sedated and home the same day.

The next step would be another chat with her oncologist to discuss further chemotherapy. In the meantime, Ronda would be thinking about it. Her consultant said she could have six rounds of carboplatin with paclitaxel – GREAT! Although this should be music to her ears, she was also dreading the thought of going through it again. The side effects from these deadly poisons, filled her with dread. At the same time, she felt lucky more chemo was an option, she was fully aware that one day, they were going to tell her, her body wouldn`t tolerate anymore. This was how it was going to be from now on and there was nothing she could do to change that.

That evening she cried in Billy`s arms, 'I don`t want any more chemo,' she said 'I don`t think I am strong enough to go through it all again.'

Billy was too choked to speak right away, but eventually he told her, selfishly, 'I want you to have it, so you can stay just one more day, but to see you go through that, will crush me.'

'Selfishly, I don`t think I can do it again,' she sobbed in his arms.

'I know, I know my darling, but if you turn it down and change your mind at a later date, you do realize, they may tell us it`s no longer an option?'

'I know that,' she said while she choked on her spital.

'If you give it a go, we can always stop mid-way, if it's too much to bear,' he told her.

The Chemotherapy would never get rid of the cancer or put it in remission, it was too wild and out of control, it was starting to get real cunning now, Ronda had a battle to kill it, the disease had a battle to stay exactly where it wanted to be, feeding from her and selfishly taking tiny bits of her each and every day. The bloody thing was thriving too well and all these poisons may offer an attempt to shrink it, but they also put Ronda's life in danger to another level. At least at the moment, she had a chance to prolong her life. Reducing the disease in size should offer more comfort, because right now the pressure of the thing feels as though she was sitting on a massive lump, which in theory that's because she was!

Ronda described it as a full-term pregnancy with the baby's head engaged, all you mummies out there will understand that feeling, 'That's how it felt, only this lump doesn`t kick,' she told her oncologist, 'I just want to give birth to it.'

Just as she was loving her new pixi style and bleached white hair, in a matter of weeks from now, it would be a heap on the pillow, she didn`t think she was strong enough to do the head shave thing again, even if it meant she could stay another day.

Looking on the positive side – she would`t need to worry about chin hair.

This would be the fourth cancelled Christmas but at least she wouldn`t be the one cooking the Turkey!

As Ronda pinched herself in the hope she would wake up from a terrible nightmare, sadly this was real, she was never sleeping.

The confirmation letter arrived in the post two days later – the date for the stents to be inserted was scheduled for the following week.

'Hang on a minute!' aghast, Ronda read out the black print **'Nephrostomy Insertion,** what the hell is that? This wasn`t what she had signed up for.

Ronda went in an over drive of panic as the shock unnerved her.

In one way this would be better because it meant the tube would be connected on the outside of her body to a catheter bag.

The stent would have been connected through the back into her kidney, down the ureter and into her bladder so she could pee normally, but it would have been a bigger procedure.

Ronda didn`t think about that, she could only compare it with being invisible or carrying the hideous urine filled bags around with her, remembering the horrors of the drain bags after her bilacteral mastectomies which she only had for the five days stay in hospital.

Pulling her big girl knickers up to chin level, she tried to accept it was only a matter of time before her battle in fighting this evil disease would be lost, she was determined not to give in easily.

*A soldier is brave as he fights for his Queen and Country – Ronda was trying to be brave to fight for her family and much loved friends . . .*

# Chapter 26

## Thursday 16th September.

This reminded Ronda of the times they set off early to the airport – but this was no holiday, it wasn`t even a walk in the park.

Ronda had never been a morning person, to be up at this hour was only under protest.

There was a fresh chill in the air as Autumn was beginning to close in. The sun still had some warmth in it by mid-day but the sun had not even broken through the mist by seven am when they set off for the City Hospital.

The traffic was busy as most people drove to work, some going towards the city and others heading away. As the sun started to show its first flicker of light as it broke through the fen land dawn mist, Ronda was blinded by its dazzle. She was feeling thankful she has no need to drive as Billy did so without complaint.

Neither of them spoke, Ronda wouldn`t hear anyway while she closed her mind into the ether, focusing on a numb emptiness. She wondered what it would be like to be another as the fat bodied spider caught her eye as he hung onto his fine thread as though his life depended on it.

It made Ronda realize that all creatures great or small have life threatening challenges. There was no escape for anything that breathed.

The fine thread clung onto the side edge of the window

mirror as it flapped at speed in the wind.

Most people would go about their daily business with decorum, and the spider would never even be noticed. The spider continued to cling on, Ronda became more and more fascinated by the strength of his thread and the determination of the spider that clung on. Ronda envied his bravery, she wasn't feeling as brave herself.

She continued to stare in wonder, expected his life line to break at any moment. But, break it did not. Ronda was aware how easily she could change his fate; it would only take a gentle wipe of her finger and the spider's plight would once and for all be over.

Ronda's thoughts wandered and from that moment she understood how vulnerable we all are, no matter who we are, what we do, or what we are about to face. The challenges to stay safe are huge. She wondered if this tiny spider felt the same fear that Ronda was feeling on that very morning, assuming the thing has a brain, he must do, to be able to survive as he was able to right now. His tiny legs must be so strong to cling on while he flapped at seventy miles an hour.

While Ronda sat at the side of her husband, safe and loved inside the comfort of the vehicle, her belly tied itself in triple knots as it swirled around like a washing machine. How can your thoughts be empty about what you are about to face, and yet be plagued by anxiety? She was clueless how to begin to describe it. The feelings came in waves over and over again as the froth engulfed her.

As they approached closer to the city, the end-to-end

traffic cruised slowly towards the next set of traffic lights. Stop, Go, Stop, Go, until it was time to indicate and turn into the hospital grounds.

Ronda's eyes turned towards the tiny creature who continued to cling to his unbroken web.

He was safe for the time being as Billy parked the car in the drop off bay, and the spider had ceased to flap against the air.

But the question was – How safe was Ronda?

Billy walked his wife to the booking in desk in the ICU and sat with her until a nurse called her name and then he was gone. This reminded her of the times her mother would leave her at the school gates in those early years.

Ronda took her tiny eight-legged friend with her as her inspiration, hoping he survived the journey home again. She told herself, if he could survive his ordeal then she would too.

The first hour passed quickly – the nurse led her to bay fourteen and from that moment she became no more than a number. A curtain was pulled across either side and the end for privacy. There was one chair for the patient and an open space for a bed.

The chair was uncomfortable after a while, its base was firm, the sides high and hard, and the back was straight. If only she could be in the same comfort as the chemotherapy chairs, she could recline and have a snooze. If only she could find comfort she would have no need to complain.

But that was okay, she wouldn't be sat too long, in the meantime she told herself she just had to make the most of it.

Once the questions on the paper had been answered, obs were taken every thirty minutes.

Everyone seemed to be nil by mouth, Ronda had taken her last sip of water at six thirty that morning. It was only eight thirty and she was already parched for a cup of tea.

The nurse asked if she had brought an over night bag with her, she told her she had and it was safely with her husband to drop off later if it was needed.

'Oh, you will be staying the night here because you are down for a general anesthetic.'

From that moment Ronda's anxieties dissolved away and she became quite relaxed.

'You are on the morning list,' the nurse told her. 'It depends where you are on the list to how long you will be waiting but it shouldn`t be too long,' she told her.

Ronda figured out that if she was last on the morning list, they may still let her go home in the evening. How could she possibly know, it would turn out so differently?

The minutes passed into hours, while she read four chapters of her book. By mid-day her eye lids felt heavy and began to blur. She turned down the corner of her page and put the book away.

The chair was high and her feet couldn`t quite reach the floor, she asked for a pillow for the small of her back. The neuropathy in her chemo damaged feet felt cold and numb, they were beginning to swell like old ladies' ankles, with a bluish tinge to them. The pins and needles in her finger ends had begun to travel towards her elbow. It was not a nice feeling. The poor circulation was not helped by the chair.

Ronda was aware of her fibromyalgia body ceasing up into one of her rigor-mortis episodes and the all-over body aches were now turning into agonizing pain.

The cancerous mass in her pelvic laid heavy on her lower spine, the pain triggered down to her knees, progressing round to her belly.

'Go for a walk,' the nurse suggested.

The nurse didn`t have a clue, Ronda was no more capable of walking a jolly down the corridor than anyone else in such pain. She stood and stretched but her feet were unable to carry her weight for long, as soon as she sat, the pain rushed through her entire body like a tornado.

Ronda's thoughts went back to the fat bodied spider, she had to be stronger than this, so she tried to draw on his courage to fight.

Things moved from bad to worse as the clock ticked past another hour. The thirst and the hunger hit another level. She hadn`t eaten for twenty hours, not a drop of fluid had passed her lips in over six hours. She was beginning to feel faint, she was hot and clammy from the pain, weak, sick and dizzy and extremely emotional. The reason she was there didn`t bear thinking about. At that moment in time, she could only think about the here and now.

The older woman in the bay opposite kept staring. At least Ronda could feel grateful she wasn`t asked to wear the dreadfully tight surgical stockings that poor lady did. Ronda was fully aware how tight and uncomfortable they were, they cut into one's flesh, so they do. The lady also had arthritic pain – Ronda felt a great deal of sympathy for her. The lady had been waiting for as many hours as Ronda. She sensed her agitation by her body language.

The same lady dared to ask the dreaded question, 'How much longer?' as the clock turned to one thirty.

The nurse snapped at her, telling her it could be as late as five! The woman was incredibly anxious and she started to cry. Ronda wanted to hug her and cry too. The nurse just walked away with no words of comfort.

The lady who sat in the bay to Ronda's right had been for her procedure and was long gone. How lucky was she. The next patient was brought through, the curtains drawn around her.

A different nurse expressed her kindness as she asked the same questions as she`d asked other patients before her.

'It`s the waiting that's the worst,` she told the nurse. She was obviously aware of the system.

The woman sitting in the bay to Ronda's left kept peeping around the curtain at her. Ronda's pain was taking her to an even higher level by now and she wasn`t feeling very sociable, so she chose to ignore her. Ronda felt the urge to pull the curtain all the way across for privacy, but that would have been rude, she wanted to tell her to 'do one,' but she didn`t of course. She kept her eyes away, she knew the minute she looked at her, the women would start a conversation. After a couple more peeps, Ronda glared at her.

'How long have you been waiting?' she asked.

'Since eight o`clock this morning,' Ronda told her.

'Oh, I`ve been here since seven thirty,' the women

tittered, as if it was a competition.

Ronda knew if the conversation continued, she would be asking what procedure she was having done and Ronda really did not want to say it, 'Piss bag,' I mean Gordon flipping Bennet!

Ronda made no comment to the fact it must be absolutely devastating to have been waiting another thirty minutes, I mean, that is bad, isn't it?

'It's not much fun, is it?' the women jested.

'Not when you're sitting on a ten-pound cancerous mass, it's not,' Ronda scoffed.

The fact Ronda had no idea how much her tumour weighed didn't even matter; she did know it was the size of a small melon so she guessed it could be a ten pounder. God knows where she was hiding the thing, because she didn't look as pregnant as she felt.

The woman didn't answer, she quickly disappeared to her own side of the curtain and never spied on her again. I don't suppose she could compete with that – no Ronda thought, she'd be one of these whingers who turns a normal headache into a migraine and then tells everyone, she has a migraine but still gets up in the morning and goes to work. Sympathy votes don't wash with Ronda anymore. She is sick to her back teeth about folk moaning about an in grown toe nail when she was going through so much shit and if that made her old and bitter, then she was old and bitter.

The lady in the opposite bay went down for her procedure, while the new lady in the bay to Ronda's right repeated the same words she had said a few times before, 'It's the waiting that's the worse,' she told every nurse, specialist, consultant who dare to venture close to hearing range.

'It's the waiting that's the worse,' she told Ronda for the fourth time.

Ronda didn't have anything nice to say, so she didn't say anything at all.

Five minutes later they came to take the woman for her procedure – she had been waiting exactly ninety minutes!

The lady opposite returned thirty minutes later and was quickly offered a nice cup of tea and a sandwich, while Ronda continued to wait.

Billy continued to call Ronda's cell phone – she was unaware that he had called the ICU to complain. She noticed a couple of nurses glancing across to her, one told the other, she had noticed Ronda had been waiting a very long time and asked the other nurse if she was alright.

The nurse asked if she was okay and Ronda told her she wasn't, she was in a great deal of pain. Of course, the nurses wouldn't know about Ronda's fibromyalgia or her cancerous mass.

The nurse offered her paracetamol but Ronda declined the offer because she just may as well take smarties and she couldn't have Ibuprofen with her dodgy kidney.

'What do you normally take?' the nurse asked.

Ronda told her she was on codeine, but she didn't think she could have the water to swallow them.

Well, one nurse said she could, another said she couldn't, another said she would have to call theatre to ask the surgeon. She also would need a doctor to sign a prescription for them and this would all take time. Ronda figured that it wouldn't really matter if she was having a general anesthetic, besides she would be given pain meds after the procedure any way - well wouldn't she?

In the meantime, one nurse phoned the theatre and she was given the okay to wet her lips enough to swallow a tablet. So Ronda asked if she could take one of her own from her bag. They said, 'NO, you'll have to wait for someone to collect the tablet from pharmacy and that could take an hour!'

Ronda told Billy all of this when he called again – the only problem was another twenty minutes had passed and she was still waiting for her water and fury hit him, he called the unit back and blew one. The same stroppy nurse who had made the lady in the bay opposite cry came charging over. She told Ronda off – taking her right back to those early primary school days.

Her attitude gave Ronda the impression it was all too much trouble for her, the nurse insinuated she was run off her feet and had lots of patients to look after. This was not true she spent too much time chatting and giggling at the nurse's station to care. Ronda took her own meds anyway and swallowed them on her spittle.

Ronda tried to keep her pecker up by telling herself, 'Not long now,' like a mantra.

Ronda had been waiting eight hours by the time they collected her for her procedure.

As if her day hadn't been bad enough – how could she possibly have any idea how terrifying the next hour was going to be.

The procedure was explained in the finest of detail – the radiologist was expected to perform the operation on both kidneys. But he was hoping she would only need them temporarily and hoped if the chemo worked its magic, the nephrostomy's could be replaced with stents after twelve weeks.

The radiologist used the ultrasound machine to decide on the most suitable point for inserting the fine plastic tube (catheter), into her back. Her skin was anaesthetized with a local anaestheticed, and a fine needle inserted into the kidney, but she was not put under by a general anesthetic or sedated, she was just given the Entonox to suck on.

When the radiologist was sure that the needle was in a satisfactory position, a fine wire was placed into the kidney, through the needle, which then enabled the plastic catheter to be positioned correctly. This catheter was then fixed to the skin surface, and attached to a drainage bag.

The pain was excruciating, it was cruel and barbaric and Ronda now had further anxieties about going through this again. It was Ronda's body but it was totally out of her hands – she had no choice but do as she was told and let the nightmare commence. It was difficult to be truly grateful, even though this was all part of saving her life.

The fact that Ronda was already in pain wasn`t helped by the position she had to lay. An extremely hard rolled up theatre towel was placed under her lower tummy while she lay on her front. This was torture in itself, the spasms in her lower back were beyond describing. She whimpered like a yelping dog, no one seemed to be in the least bit perturbed. She took deep breaths on the Entonox just how she remembered three and a half decades ago when she was in labour with Bella. But these pains didn`t come and go in waves they continued to screw her up to a higher level and instead of taking deep breaths she wanted to hold them in.

She had been aware of the bright lights even though she had closed her eyes. Then suddenly she panicked as the light faded and took her into a deep blackness. For a short second she thought she had died. She opened her eyes in a rush, to find the light had only been dimmed.

She felt the sting of the needle as it punctured her flesh, but the pain didn`t fade it only intensified as it was pushed into her back and into her kidney. She sucked so hard, again, again and again, but as soon as she stopped the pain quickly returned.

'Nice deep breaths, tubes passing through now.'

'Nice and still,' he told her, 'otherwise you will move the kidney.'

'It hurt so much with each deep breath she wasn`t sure whether to risk it again.

When it was over the pain didn`t waver, it was awful. But thank God it was over! Although it wasn`t, was it? This was just the beginning of The End. . .

# Chapter 27

## `A surprised phone call`

All told, Tuesday was a harrowing day – after a morning at the dentist, followed by an afternoon having her nephrostomy bag and dressing changed, a blood test at the Johnson's Hospital, Ronda went home and took herself straight off to bed.

Back downstairs to watch the soaps, the land line phone rang at exactly 7.30, as the music from Emmerdale closed the program. Only scam callers dialed the house number. Who could it be?

'Hello, 01755 724110'

'Good evening, It's Peterborough City Hospital, I am one of the oncologist nurses, can I please speak to Mrs Ronda Stone?'

'Yes, Ronda speaking,' she told the voice the other end of the telephone.

'Oh, hello Ronda, I am so sorry to be calling so late in the day, it's Paula here from oncology.'

'Hello Paula, I thought I recognized the voice.'

'I am looking at today's blood test results,' she said, 'your platelets are seriously low, my lovely, and we need you to pack an over-night bag and come over to Peterborough City Hospital as soon as possible.'

'WHY?'

'We need to give you a platelet transfusion.'

'What, NOW?'

'Unfortunately, yes my darling.'

'Can I not have a good night's sleep in my own bed and come over first thing in the morning?'

'No, it's far too urgent I'm afraid, we need to keep an eye on you through the night, just to make sure you don't have a serious bleed.

'A bleed! bleed where?'

'Regrettably you are at a very high risk of a brain bleed,'

'Really, it's that serious?'

'I'm afraid I don't want to worry you – but, yes, it is serious.'

'Is this chemo related?'

'I'm afraid it is, but it is fixable and we'd rather not wait until the morning,'

'I suppose I have no choice then?'

'We can't force you, but we strongly advise that you do.'

'Okay, we will be there as soon as possible.'

'Come straight to the emergency department and don't queue, someone from oncology will be there waiting for you. Just flash your chemo emergency card and wait as far away from other patients as possible.

Ronda and Billy didn't utter a word for the thirty-minute journey. Ronda felt panicky, not over the procedure, but because she really did not want to spend hours in the A & E department of the hospital – maybe isolated in a brightly lit room with no windows, in other words a box, or more to the point on one of those awful trolley beds. Knowing she had no choice in the matter, she prayed it wouldn't be so bad as other times.

Nine blood tests later and two culture tests, never ending intravenous antibiotics, blood pressure, temperature, and so forth, Ronda found a little sleep by two o'clock in the morning.

The unit was so incredibly busy and loud, it was difficult to even find rest at all, in spite of the welcomed air mattress, the oncology nurse had kindly found for her ready and waiting.

Ronda became aware of her own body jerking as her nerves started to relax. A sudden jump brought Ronda back to consciousness, followed by the whole process repeating itself. A faint voice disturbed her, 'Ronda, I need to do your obs darling.'

Another bleep in her ear, to find a normal temperature. The pinch on her arm from the blood pressure monitor offered a normal reading.

Was all this really necessary at such a God earthly hour of the morning?

'It`s protocol,' Ronda told herself.

The experience was a nightmare, if she felt well on arrival she sure as hell didn`t now.


Just as Ronda was losing the will, the department livened up. Four muscular prison officers came in with an in-mate chained to his ankle and another's wrist.

From the moment he arrived he caused mayhem, he was gobby, loud and clearly attention seeking.

He complained of a long list of ailments. He was tested, x-rayed, scanned, he had an ECG – all of which was fine. He added new symptoms all through the night, making new demands for a brain scan because of a headache that had magically developed a few hours after his arrival.

Basically, he was just having a laugh, there was nothing wrong with him at all, he just wanted to escape on a jolly in the early hours of a Wednesday morning.

He was proudly telling stories about the naughty things he had got away with in his youth, all petty crime but to him it made him a hero.

He soon became exhausted by the sound of his own voice, but it wasn`t long after he became bored and agitated, demanding to have the handcuffs removed so he could use the loo in privacy. The officers weren`t falling for that trick, four of them escorted him to the toilet under the prisoner's protest.

On their return two of the prison officers went on a break, leaving just the two. The prisoner used this opportunity to kick off about wanting his hand cuffs removed.

He made out his arthritic hip was giving him pain and he needed to lay on the opposite side.

'Please man, just take the fucking cuffs off, its not like I'm going to do a runner or anyfink,' he chanted.

'You know I can`t do that.'

'Come on mate, I promise I won`t do nuffing stupid.'

'You can kick off all you like, it ain`t `appening, end of.'

'Oh man, who the fuck will know? Just undo the fucking cuffs.'

It went quiet for a while, but the entertainment prevented Ronda from closing her eyes in spite of the fact she needed her rest.

'Oh man, I am in so much pain – please just swap the cuffs onto the other side so I can turn over.'

'No can-do sunshine.'

'Bastard, bastard, bastard,' he chanted 'This is fucking inhumane, please, please I am in agony here man.'

The prison officer ignored his plight.

'Okay then, I am going to turn over anyway!'

Knowing this would cause a great deal more discomfort for both of them, the prisoner yanked the officer's arm across his own wide body as he turned onto the opposite side. The officer was left stretching his arm across in the most dreadful position. The officer kept his calm in the matter, which seemed to provoke the prisoner even more.

Everything after that seemed to happen very quickly, 'Police, police, police – someone call the police, I have been sexually assaulted,' the prisoner yelled out loud.

It was a while before anyone responded – for heaven's sake they had real life and death situations to attend to, but eventually a doctor came.

'Now what's the problem Malcolm?' as though the doctor was only too familiar with the ten ton, tattooed fatty.

'It's 'im bro, he just sexually assaulted me.'

'Do you wish to make an informal complaint?' the doctor asked unperturbed.

'Of course, I fucking do bro, he grabbed my fucking bollocks man,'

'You saying he interfered with your testicles?' he asked the question with a great deal of doubt.

'Yer man, I am in so much pain in my knackers man, he wouldn't take the fucking cuffs off so I could roll over, and when I did anyway, he grabbed and squeezed me hard, if yah know what I mean.'

'Was it a tight squeeze?' the doctor asked trying not to break a smile.

'What do you mean? He touched me up, the pervy fucker, good and proper – I tell you until my eyes watered.'

'So, you are making a physical complaint as well as a sexual one?'

'Well, I ain`t making the fucker up, am I doc – just phone the fucking police will ya, I `ave a crime to report.'

The doctor walked away making no further comment, and no one phoned the police.

The prisoner continued to form a complaint to every Tom, Dick and Harry who cared to listen, although he was bringing far too much attention to himself no one took a blind bit of notice.

It was hard for Ronda to ignore him while her bed was directly opposite his, unless she closed her eyes it was difficult not to stare.

'Eh love, you must have seen what `appened, can you phone the police?'

'Sorry, didn`t see anything.'

'Well, you can phone the police for me, can`t you?'

'Not a chance,' Ronda chuckled 'there's no signal down here,' she correctly told him.

The show didn`t last much longer after that but it kept Ronda entertained for a few hours. Of course, there was absolutely nothing wrong with Malcolm. He left with a clean bill of health – but what a waste of NHS money.

Although Ronda had spent twenty-three hours in Accident and Emergency the air mattress was gratefully received and she wasn`t too worse for wear.

An hour later she was moved to the oncology ward for her platelet transfusion. She was at last comfortable in isolation while they started to treat her for sepsis. She had no idea she was here to stay for a week or a day.

One of the benefits of having one's own room was it gave Ronda much needed rest and she had a fabulous wet room all to herself.

Ronda was finding the hot water and bubbles of shower gel soothing enough to groan with pleasure as she washed and conditioned her hair.

As she switched off the water and reached for the towel, she heard the death curdling scream of panicked nurses the other side of her bathroom door. When she pulled back the shower curtain, she noticed her slippers floating towards the lavatory and a tidal wave of bubbles heading for the door. Ronda stared with wide eyes as water ran under the gap at the bottom, it was instinct to open the door. Oh my God, it was like a flash flood, Ronda's bedroom was like a flipping duck pond.

'No, don`t come out yet,' the nurses chided in unison.

'Shit,' was all Ronda could say.

An even louder kerfuffle could be heard as far away as the nurses' station while the water ran over their shoes.

By the time the water had drained from the bathroom floor, Ronda suspected the panic was over. She gingerly opened a crack in the door to check out the damage. Four nurses shuffled on some towels to soak up the moisture.

*'Oh my days, it could only happen to Ronda'*

Ronda, had no real idea how poorly she was, as well as

having a platelet transfusion, she was treated for sepsis; had two ECG`s; one chest x-ray; intravenous anti-biotics; injections in her tummy for her low immunity; medication for magnesium deficiency and phosphate deficiency; mouth rinse with and gelclair for the thirty-two blisters in her mouth; twenty-three hours of intravenous hydration; three cannulas ran frequently side by side: She was treated for pain in her nephrostomy site, ultra sound scans on her kidneys, two covid tests and one MRSA test.

Ronda's hospital stay was rather enlightening to say the least but grim it really was not. . . . or at least not all of the time.

By the Friday, Ronda was moved into a shared ward with a total of five beds. It was actually nice to have some company.

Caroline had been diagnosed with cerebral palsy at the grand age of seventy years. She was now seventy-six, her relapse had put her in hospital. 'I really shouldn`t be here,' she told them, 'because I don`t have cancer. Infact I shouldn`t be here at all really, people with cerebral palsy don`t live until they are my age, but there is no special ward for the disease.'

Caroline was an interesting lady, she told stories of her life that inspired us, in spite of her difficulties that had not been given a diagnosis, she explained that her version of the disease was rather mild and until now she had been able to manage the disease with a gutsy determination.

Ronda was finding one cannula clumsy enough but three was beyond a joke. Nurses came, nurses went as shifts changed, they all asked the question, 'Why do you have three cannulas? I will take two of them out,' they would say.

The third nurse that mentioned it actually did it right away, 'One, two, three,' she said and out it came, but blood spurted everywhere, a shower covered the nurse, Ronda, the bedding.

'Well, anyone wanting a quick suicide, I guess that's the way to do it?' Ronda joked.

Once the drama was over, Caroline quipped, 'I guess she had no idea your platelets are low then?'

'We couldn`t make it up, could we,' Ronda agreed.

'I know,' Caroline continued, 'last week I bleeped the nurse for the bed pan, the nurse took so long coming, I shit the bed – followed by a second explosion when she rolled me over to clear up the mess, shit everywhere, all over her uniform. She wasn`t quite sure who or what to clean up first.

'I told her when nature calls it waits for no man, there was crap everywhere,' she scoffed.

Betty was a dear little lady, she had a frail, skeletal frame which made you want to wrap her up in cotton wool, otherwise she may break. Like Caroline she was unable to get out of bed. Betty was desperate to go home but clearly, she needed a good nursing home. She had advanced Parkinson's disease and was rarely able to communicate with anyone.

Jill was eighty-two, unable to get out of bed because she had broken her ankle and her surgery to place twelve screws had not healed. Like Ronda, Jill was treated for sepsis, she also had secondary breast cancer in her lung, like Ronda incurable.

Caroline and Jilly made their feelings clear, they had had enough suffering they were ready to go to the pearly gates.

'I`ve had enough' she told Ronda, 'What is the point in this?'

It was unusual for Ronda to be lost for words, but she felt so sad she had no idea what to say to her. The thing was, she well and truly partly understood.

When Jill`s machine started to bleep, the hazard light flashed. From Ronda`s experience of the chemo clinic this often happened when the drip had finished or the patient had moved their arm. But when no one came, and Ronda noticed blood in Jill's tube, she took it upon herself to ring her own buzzer. By the time the nurses came, Jill and Ronda were in hysterics laughing.

'Oh I am so sorry,' Ronda told her, 'I rang my bell because Jill couldn`t find hers, the bleeping wouldn`t stop and I noticed the blood in her tube Sorry,' Ronda said again, 'I have only just realized she is having a blood transfusion.'

The ward filled with an eruption of laughter and from that day forward there was never a dull moment.

Then there was Emma who chose to keep her curtains drawn. At nine o'clock she had a very loud conversation with her husband and three children on speaker phone. The conversation was mostly spoken in perfect English with no identifiable accent. Occasionally she spoke in another tongue that was not recognizable.

The call ended an hour and ten minutes later. She came over as head-strong, selfish with no consideration of these poorly ladies who clearly needed to rest. Is there any wonder, they were ready for the land of the Gods.

By the end of the phone call, she was munching on crisps, opening packets and screwing them up. Her locker doors opened, closed, opened again, bags rattled, cans were sprayed loudly. Ronda was unable to give into the exhaustion she felt. She had a great need to rest but sleep never came.

Eventually Emma's bright light that reflected on the ceiling behind the closed curtain dimmed, but the disturbance she created did not waver. She started to preach the gospel out loud in a language Ronda struggled to recognize.

Caroline asked her to say a prayer for her too, 'I`m ready to go to the Angels,' Caroline told her. Ronda understood what she meant as she was losing the will herself. The tiredness provoked her, but she said nothing.

Ronda could not quite put her finger on her colour, race or creed.

The following morning Emma went home and only then did Ronda greet her with a brief hello, goodbye in one . . . . It was only then did Ronda discover her true identity, Emma was a beautiful Nigerian women in her early forties.

The lady who moved into Emma's bay was a young white woman who was clearly poorly. It was also her preference to hide behind her curtain. She was well spoken and chatty enough with the nurses but she did not want to interact with the other patients at all, most probably too embarrassed to show her face after so much grunting and force farting behind her curtain. If she wasn`t farting loudly she was belching or eating loudly.

When the dinner lady took their order, she ordered more grub than the other four ladies put together.

Ronda expected her to be obese, and obese she was indeed.

Between them, Caroline, Rachel and Betty snored like twenty dozen hogs at the pig market.

One would guarantee each time the dinner lady brought lunch or dinner, would the buzzers begin to bleep. One, two, three in unision, 'I need the bed pan,' leaving Jill and Ronda retching on their sandwich or soup and each mouthful became too difficult to contemplate.

'Why do they always need a shit, just as we are about to eat,' Jill said tersely.

Ronda belly laughed as she remembered the story of their cat.

Sharing her story with Jill, 'This cat broke his little toe and was put in a plaster cast, we borrowed a large dog pen to confine him from climbing the stairs or jumping on the furniture.

'Now, that cat could stay in a whole day and a night and all the next day and never ask to go out to the toilet, but you could guarantee each time the family sat down at the kitchen table to eat, that ruddy Tom cat decided to have a shit in his litter tray.'

Jill and Ronda were floored with laughter and wet eyes, while the other's remained totally oblivious their joke was on them.

One bell buzzed, 'Done,' a voice spoke behind the curtain of bay twenty.

'Done,' spoke another.

'Done,' shouted another – while Jill and Ronda shared their own humour.

'What are you two finding so funny to giggle about?' Caroline scoffed.

'Shall I tell her or will you?' Jilly teased.

'Absolutely nothing for you to worry about,' Ronda assured her with a deep stare at Jilly as if to tell her, 'Don`t you dare.'

In spite of Ronda`s nephrostomy insertion she also needed to pee normally from her right kidney. She was the only one who was able to get out of bed, she was mobile enough to shower, and care for her own personal toilet needs.

She had named her infusion machine Derek the Dalek and like it or not Derek went everywhere with her. Ronda planned her showers in between the intravenous infusions to give her the freedom to do so, while Derek waited at her bedside.

On the way back from the bathroom to bed there always seemed to be one of her new friends in need. Either to find the buzzer to bleep the nurse, or help them to operate the height of their own bed. Ronda did not mind at all, in fact it made her feel lucky to be useful. It helped her appreciate her own mobility.

Jilly was having a really bad down-day – 'I`m ready to go,' she told anyone in hearing range.

'Go home, Jilly?' Ronda asked curiously.

'No, I don`t want to go home.'

'Then where Jilly, where do you want to go?'

'To the Angels,' she cried. 'What is the point to all of this? It`s not living it's just existence.' She said in a shaky voice while her emotions overwhelmed her.

'I know darling,' Ronda had a great need to sit by her bedside and hold her hand but of course it wasn`t allowed, not while covid was around. Ronda felt a teary eye sting, she had no words but she knew exactly how Jilly felt.

No one spoke for a while – then suddenly Jilly cheered, pointing to the floor like an excited child, 'Look Ronda, look, a white feather.'

Ronda shuffled out of bed, struggling with Derek to take a closer look, it made her smile as she bent to pick it up and pass the small piece of white plastic to Jill.

Ronda, laughed as she handed it to her, 'You're as bad as my daughter, she is always finding white feathers, thinks it's her granddad,'

'Oh,' Jilly whimpered, 'how lovely.'

'Daft bugger, I tell her she will find white feathers, it's because all her bloody cushions and pillows are filled with white fluffy feathers.

'You not a believer then?' Caroline chided incredulously.

'I am, but lets face it there is a flipping limit.' Pointing to the jug of water on Caroline's table, she told her, 'It's like this Caroline, as hard as I try I could not make your jug of water move across to Jilly's table, as long as I lived with an active brain, so I ain't going to be able to do it when I am dead – now am I?'

'I like your logic . . . BUT!'

'There is no BUT about it, I tell you it can't 'appen,'

By the end of the conversation even Ronda had convinced herself the after life did in actual fact exist! which led her to her first book, "RONDA' Back in the day."

While Ronda intrigued her new audience, the ladies became rather excited . . .

'Oh, I must read your book,' Caroline told her, is it

available on kindle or audio?'

'I`m afraid not,' Ronda explained, mainly because of the cost to the author, it would cost me three thousand pounds to have the privilege of those options, and the profit to myself is as low as a pound for every book the seller sells for me.'

'I feel excited,' Jilly said, 'I`ve never met an author before.'

'Well, if you ladies are up for a bed time read later, I will ask my Billy to bring in a copy that I can read out loud to you.'

'Oh, would you?' Caroline asked, 'That would be marvellous.'

So, that is what happened.


The following evening Jilly was agitated by her bed remote control.

'Ronda,' she asked, 'how do I get my bed to move down?'

'Oh, my God,' Ronda gasped as she glanced across to Jilly`s bay, to discover her bed was so high in the air she was almost stuck on the ceiling.

'Flipping heck Jilly, how on earth did you get so high up in the ruddy air like that?'

'I don`t know,' she cried.

'Click the down arrow on the third diagram.'

'That`s what I am doing, but it's only moving the table down.'

'What do you mean, the table?'

'The table moves up and down but not the bed.'

'Jill darling, it`s the remote control for the bed – your table can`t possibly move up or down, unless you do it manually by the switch at the end of the table.'

'But it is, look.'

Ronda watched patiently, laughing she told Jilly her bed was indeed moving down.

'No, it's not, but my table is Watch.'

'I am watching Jilly, and I can assure you your bed is moving up and down accordingly.'

'But what about my table? Its moving up and down.'

'It`s an illusion darling, it's not the table that's moving its your bed.'

Well, Jilly wasn`t having any of it! Then Caroline chided – 'Jill is correct you know, I can see her table moving from the other side of the room.'

Ronda was beginning to think these ladies were beyond help still seeing the funny side she said, 'Now, don`t you start,' with a loud belly laugh.

'Well, I can`t get my bed as low as yours,' Caroline insisted.

'Yes you can.'

'No I can`t, no matter how hard I try my table will never be level with my bed, like yours is.'

'That's probably because your table is a lot lower than mine.'

And so, the banter continued . . .

'Oh, I can`t be bothered anymore, who cares anyway, I`m knackered,' Caroline stated grumpily.

But Ronda couldn`t settle – let alone stop laughing. The bewildered look on Jilly`s face said it all, 'All I want is my bed to go lower,'

Ronda decided no one was going to find sleep that night, so she took it upon her exhausted self to unplug Derek and drag him across to Jill`s bed side. She procceeded her demonstration by removing Jill's table away from her bed and lined it parallel to her own.

'Right-i-ho, this is your table and this is mine, they are both at the same height,' she shuffled across to Caroline's bed and wheeled her table to line up with the others, asking Caroline to take note that her table was indeed lower than the other two.

'So, here we have it – three tables lined neatly in the centre space of the room. Now, watch Jill`s table as she operates the down button on the remote control.'

The two ladies did as Ronda instructed. Nothing happened, 'Now, keeping your eye on the tables watch as Jill operates the up button,' again nothing happened.

'Well, it ain`t doing it now,' Jilly said adamantly.

'That's because the remote control is for the bed – not the bloody table,'

Jilly and Ronda laughed real tears so much so, they each bleeped for the nurse for some pain killers.

'What on earth is going on in here?' We can hear you partying down the flipping corridor.

'Oh, please tell them these remote controls do not operate the tables.'

'Of course not,' Gemma explained. . . 'they operate the bed.'

'THANK YOU,' Ronda belly laughed. 'Now, take your eyes away from the tables and focus on the ceiling - Jilly operate the down button, Caroline operate the up button.' and indeed both ladies managed to position their own bed to the right height.

'Oh, yer, well I never,' Jilly said. 'You are right Ronda,'

'YESSSSSS,' Ronda huffed. 'At-flipping-last.'

Caroline grunted and rolled over because she wasn`t used to being wrong for once in her life.

Once they were back on the sleeping pills, they soon settled down – but with Ronda there was always more.

'Ronda,' Jilly cooed, 'how do we operate the table?'

'There is a lever on the side, you pull it up manually to go higher and press it down to go lower'

'Oh, only my table is different to yours, mine doesn`t have a lever.'

'That's because my table is facing the other way to yours,'

'Oh yes,'

'Gordon-flipping-Bennett,' Ronda quoted with another giggle.

'I haven`t heard that saying in a long while, the nurse chuckled.'

'You shouldn`t swear,' Caroline chided.

'It`s not swearing Caroline, it`s to replace swear words,' Ronda corrected.

'Who is Gordon Bennett anyway?'

'I don`t know, I will google it,' Ronda offered.

'In the morning – please can we go to sleep now,'

Pause . . . .

'Found it - The phase came from a real person whose name was Gordon Bennett.

The term of phase was used to replace swear words,' 'in other words, we say it instead of saying 'for fucks sake.'

The following Monday Ronda`s oncologist came to the ward to tell her the good news, 'You are going home.'

'Today?'

'Yes, today, the not so good news I have booked you an appointment for a blood transfusion next week.'

Then came the next blow, she was fit for chemo on the Friday.

Panic hit her, no it`s too soon, I need more time, what if it puts me right back in hospital?

'I will be reducing your dose considerably,' she told her and then she was gone.

# Epilogue

Ronda cries with exhaustion, as her profound fatigue is the worst she has ever endured.

'I am just about to get up, having a cuppa and then I must embrace the day, what`s left of it. I can`t do much, my body is too weak and thin while next week it starts all over again with blood tests as I brace myself for the results and more decisions.'

It all feels as though it's closing in on her now. I think this is the beginning of the downhill spiral, as she stares at the huge bottle of morphine knowing, thinking, is this really it? As Ronda tries to prepare and accept, she continues to tell herself, 'Next week, when I feel better,' when realistically it can only get worse.

What is now part of her everyday living as she bathes in the stinging nettles, her eyeballs feel exposed and sore, as the eyelashes fade away, along with her eyebrows

A huge price to pay, but so worth it for eight years remission. But, now! What about NOW?

Even the joys of life have disintegrated bit by bit, little by little.

While the neuropathy takes hold and prevents her from doing the simplest of tasks, like reading, sewing, gluing, knitting, crochet, creating absolutely nothing. Ronda is right to think, time is urgent, because it will very soon run out. It explains why this need to get everything done is so important while she tells herself, 'I have to - I must.'

She lies in her bed staring across the fenland into the sunshine, wondering what she would do today - if she could.

Go out. - Where would she go?

How far? Who would she see?

If she went shopping, what would she buy? What would she need and why?

She tells herself, 'NOTHING! I need NOTHING!'

'I need to go nowhere, see no-one.'

'I just feel numb!'

She can't kiss, hug, cry with any one. She might catch covid, it's not safe out there. Is anyone safe?

'Gold - that's what I need, gold tissue paper to wrap the presents, the Christmas presents. But that has been taken away from us again this year . . . Christmas.'

When people tell you there is nothing to fear from dying. Well, they lie, they know nothing – how can they unless they have already died before.

THIS is dying there is nothing beautiful or peaceful about it. It is what it is and nothing can change the outcome!

The words 'Do not resuscitate,' are spoken loudly within her soul, what good can any of that do, do, do . . . ? **I am BROKEN . . .**

**Ronda's last words . . .**

*"When I was a little girl, we went to the cemetery a lot and I remember the strong aroma of the beautiful fresh flowers laid on each new grave mound. Of course, they were beautiful, its how I thought death would be, of course these people would have been buried and they knew not.*

*In life I didn't have many freshly cut flowers in a vase in my window because of my allergy's. So, I have decided to demand them in death, I don't care how much they cost. So, that will be everyone told, worry not – that is just my weird sense of humour.*

*A solid white coffin made from resin, none of this whicker shit where the worms and rats can get in.*

*I was thinking about donating my body to science until I watched silent Witness.*

*Billy wants to burn me – I keep begging him not too . . . I either want a BIG grand funeral with horse drawn carriages to represent my love of horses as a child who attended Miss Crusts riding school.*

*Or I don't want a funeral at all – I don't care either way but no viewings – everyone need to remember me with the love of life not dead in some mortuary. If anyone came to look at me, I might just sit up and bite them.*

*It will be an invitation only kind of do . . . I am setting a new trend, I want no one singing for me, it will spoil the songs. But you are welcome to come fourth and dance. As long as its not on my grave".*

Thoughts of the day by Teena Joyce - written as a blog for Ovarian Cancer UK

**Comments from our readers: -**

*Adele*
`Amazing writing. `

*Joanna*
`This breaks my heart, but I get it. You write so beautifully and from the heart. I am sure everyone can relate to this. `

*Lynn*
`Amazing words. `

*Gaynor*
`Beautifully written, from the heart`

*Margaret Obrien*
`Heartbreaking, but so realistic. `

*Katy*
`You have put into words what I made such a clumsy attempt to do last week . . . . thank you. Sending you solidarity with a big hug, we hear you, we feel you. We are in this too. `

*Wendy*
`Thank you for writing this so beautifully, your words have touched my heart. `

*Hilary*
`Beautiful words, eloquently expressed and such a

tough situation, squishy teal hugs. `

*Sarah*
`Your words, your openness has really resonated with me. Thank you for expressing your deep inner thoughts and emotions - how sincere. `

*Michelle*
`What wonderful words . . . You had me all emotional, as I know exactly how these feel, I`m with you. `

*Joan*
`So well written. `

*Jackie*
`Absolutely sums this whole shitty world of cancer, now added to the mix is covid! Well done, such a fantastic piece of writing.

*Barbara*
`The most honest, soul wrenching thing I've ever read.

*Jane*
`Made me cry, never before has someone hit it on the head with words "I`m broken."

*Gillian*
`Wow, your words, no matter what stage we are at, ruing a deep resonant bell within us all. Thank you for sharing. `

. . . .

Sadly, some of these ladies haven`t made it and others

may not - but their comments touched me in a way no one else ever could because with regret they knew Ronda, as well as she knew herself.

Cancer effects everyone in one way or another, many have been through it, while others go through it and sadly many of them will not make it.

This dreadful disease gave me the need to write Ronda's story, how she lost her dearest beloved mother with ovarian cancer, at the age of forty-seven.

Then in later years her brother, who passed away with colon cancer at the age of fifty-seven. Ronda's challenge to stay safe for as long as she could, continued for several years before she had to face it head on in the best possible way she knew how.

But, with modern medical science treatments advance every single day. They may not have found a cure or anti-dote as yet, but we have to believe they will, one day. People can live a good life with cancer, for longer than anyone could ever expect.

My words to you all, is 'NEVER GIVE UP HOPE!'